We cracked heads. . .

I heard James's startled grunt, then felt his hands beneath my elbows, lifting me up.

'Kate. . . Kate, I'm so sorry!' His breath was tickling my face.

'So am I,' I said with feeling. He was touching my forehead, fingertips gentle as they moved across my brow.

'It was such an unequal contest.' The corners of his mouth twitched upwards a little. 'I've a thicker head than yours!'

Dear Reader,

Babies loom large this month! Lilian Darcy takes us to the Barossa Valley vineyards in Australia and an obstetric practice, while Margaret Holt's second book takes us back to the midwifery unit at Beltonshaw Hospital. Two aspects of general practice are dealt with by Laura MacDonald and Janet Ferguson, though single doctor practices must be rare now! Hope you like them. . .

The Editor

Janet Ferguson was born at Newmarket, Suffolk. She nursed as a VAD during the Second World War, then became a medical secretary working in hospital in London and the provinces, and now in Brighton near her home. She has had a number of novels published, but she finds Medical Romances the most satisfying and interesting to plot.

Recent titles by the same author:

OPTICAL ILLUSION
ENCOUNTER WITH A SURGEON

THE DOCTORS AT SEFTONBRIDGE

VW

BY

JANET FERGUSON

MILLS & BOON LIMITED
ETON HOUSE   18–24 PARADISE ROAD
RICHMOND   SURREY   TW9 1SR

*First published in Great Britain 1992
by Mills & Boon Limited*

© Janet Ferguson 1992

*Australian copyright 1992
Philippine copyright 1992
This edition 1992*

ISBN 0 263 77845 2

*Set in 10 on 12 pt Linotron Times
03-9209-58830*

*Typeset in Great Britain by Centracet, Cambridge
Made and printed in Great Britain*

CHAPTER ONE

AFTER delivering Uncle John's medical article to the *Lancet* offices I took a taxi to Old Compton Street, as I was running out of time, and Nick, my fiancé, like most men, abhorred having to wait.

It was February, with sleet in the wind, and the contrasting warmth of the restaurant into which I presently stepped from the skiddy pavement outside caused nearly as much of a shock to my system as the sight of the man standing in the cocktail lounge, just to the right of the stairs.

It wasn't that he was outstandingly handsome—not in the film-star sense—but he was the kind of man to draw the eye, being tall and lean, with a good breadth to his shoulders, and the kind of demeanour that seemed to denote a natural and quiet confidence.

The plushly carpeted stairs, I knew, led up to the cloakrooms, so he was obviously waiting for someone, just as I was waiting for Nick, who hadn't yet come—a quick scan of the lounge very soon told me that. Oh, well, no matter, I thought—I'll go and leave my coat, then come back down and order myself a drink.

I had to pass near the man by the stairs, and I felt him glance at me as I put my hand on the balustrade, then I saw the girl coming down. 'Sorry to be such an age,' she called, and of course she was talking to him. She had hair the same colour as mine, only hers was short and puffed; she was trendy-plus, and her perfume stung my nose. I passed her on the wide stairs, and on glancing back as I reached the landing I saw her slip her arm through the man's, then the two of them went into the dining-room.

She was probably, I thought, as I took off my coat and rinsed my hands at one of the basins, around twenty years old—seven years younger than me. Carefully I scrutinised my face in the mirror for any sign of early wrinkles—not that I wanted to be twenty again with all those exams still to pass. I looked pale; I'd left home in a rush that morning, straight after surgery. Home for the next few months was Seftonbridge, the university town where I was living with my uncle and aunt at the Larches, River Road. Uncle John was Dr Chalmers, which was my title as well. I was a locum in his practice for three months, while his permanent partner, Rose Spender, was on maternity leave. I had been with him a week, and I fitted the post; I couldn't help knowing I did. This thought made me smile, and I saw that my lipstick needed renewing. It was a fairly discreet lipstick, for I have the kind of hair that my friends call 'Titian' and others dub 'strawberry blonde'. My eyes are green and long like a cat's, and I'm the same height as Nick, which is five foot eight when I'm wearing my highest heels. Teetering carefully down the stairs on those same heels five minutes later, I was relieved to see Nick pushing his way round the revolving doors. The shoulders of his dark city suit were sprinkled with sleet, as was the front of his hair, and I saw him pass his hand over it. Nick was fair, with smooth, even features, and hazel-brown eyes deeply set under curving brows a shade darker than his hair. And yes, he was handsome, he had always been handsome, even as a boy. I could still see the boy in him, which was probably why I loved him, or one of the reasons, anyway. I went forward to greet him; he smiled and we kissed, and all was right with my world.

'Sorry I'm late——' he brushed at his shoulders and smoothed his hair again '—but my senior partner grabbed me at exactly the wrong moment.' Nick was a partner in a well-known firm of architects in the West End, and lunching—as apart from lunching clients— wasn't all that easy for him. I had to admit, though, that I *did* wonder why he had asked me today, for we were meeting tonight, anyway; we were going to a party with my aunt and uncle in Grange Road, Seftonbridge.

As we went through into the dining-room—we had dispensed with a pre-lunch drink—I spotted the tall man and his red-haired girlfriend at a banquette table, talking animatedly together, and dipping something in sauce. Nick and I were seated at a table some distance away. The L-shaped room was packed with business-men, with only a sprinkling of women. There was a continuous hum of conversation, and a mouthwatering smell of roast meats as domed covers were lifted from trolleys and the white-aproned carver got to work.

Nick and I had soup, and baked trout with almonds, and a bottle of the house wine. Nick told me about a new hospital, currently being planned, which, if all the various permissions were granted, would eventually be erected on the site of an old hotel at Hampstead, not far from the famous Pond. It wasn't unusual for him to discuss his work, and I was always interested, but this morning I had a feeling, as I sat there drinking my wine, that he was leading up to something else, was preparing the ground for another issue that had nothing to do with blueprints or final plans. I was just about to halt him in mid-flow, and ask what was bugging him, when my attention was caught by a black-bearded man rising from a table where he'd been sitting with five other men, all guffawing loudly, drinking out of balloon glasses and smoking fat cigars. The guffawing and drinking was still going on, but Blackbeard wasn't doing it, and something about the way he was standing brought me to my feet. He was swaying, his face was contorted, his right hand moved to his left shoulder and clamped there, the fat cigar rolled down his front. The next second he was on the floor, overturning his chair, and I was running the gamut of half a dozen tables, till I dropped to my knees at his side.

He was grey-faced, pupils fixed and dilated; there was no carotid pulse. I heard myself shout, 'Someone get an ambulance—cardiac arrest!' I was aware of tables being moved, of a space being cleared, as I raked around in the patient's mouth for debris or false teeth. Then, lying on the floor at right-angles to him, I extended his neck and jaw, opened his mouth wider, fitted mine to it, making a seal of our lips, closed his nostrils with my left hand, then blew down into his lungs.

As I raised my head to take in more air, I saw kneeling opposite me the tall man who'd stood by the stairs, 'Carry on, I'll help,' he said. His hand was feeling the patient's neck, then he gave his lower sternum three chops with the heel of his hand, the force of which made me flinch. But there was still no pulse, and once more I bent. . .and sealed. . .and blew again . . .and came up for air, and down again. Breathe, damn you, breathe, I silently urged the patient, but he did nothing for himself.

My helper began cardiac compressions, and clearly knew what he was doing. 'Fifteen to two,' he instructed me quietly, and I knew what he meant—fifteen

compressions to two inflations, so right at the end of
the fifteenth downward thrust of his hands I was ready
with my own breath—blowing. . .blowing. . .blowing
. . .blowing. . .my ribs were beginning to ache.

We repeated the pattern twice after that, and then,
oh, glory, that slothful heart picked up and began to
beat by itself. Both my helper and I could feel a pulse—
flickering, it was true, erratic and not strong by any
means, but a pulse for all that. 'Give him one more
inflation, he's still not breathing on his own,' my helper
said.

I bent down and did so, and when I next came up to
draw in more used restaurant air the ambulancemen
were there with their stretcher and breathing apparatus.
My assistant was on his feet giving short, sharp details.
I heard him say he was a doctor, which didn't surprise
me a bit. In no time at all the patient, whose name
turned out to be Alex Raunds, was reassured, and
carried out to the ambulance. One of his lunch com-
panions—clearly very upset—went with him to the
Middlesex hospital.

No sooner had they gone than a bevy of waiters put
the tables back into place and produced clean cloths
and cutlery, while one or two people near by said, 'Well
done!' to me.

'I second that,' said my doctor assistant, who was
taking me back to Nick.

'You did the hardest part,' I laughed, not that I felt
like laughing for my legs were jelly; the aftermath of
trauma always went to my knees.

'Are you a nurse?' he asked me, 'or just a first aid
buff?'

'Neither, I'm a doctor, and I know you are, I heard
you say so just now.'

'Then our Mr Raunds was lucky, wasn't he? He fell into capable hands.' There was an element of surprise in his voice, and I got the impression that he might have questioned me further, but by this time we had reached Nick, who was standing at our table, looking flushed and disturbed. 'Your friend needs a good stiff drink.' Doctor Whoever he was let go of my arm to shake my hand and, meeting his eyes, my legs went more useless than ever, and I was glad to sit down while he went off to join his red-haired friend.

'I didn't know whether to come over or not. Is the man dead?' Nick asked.

'I hope not, after all that effort.' I felt messy and very hot. I had a burning desire to sluice my face and do something to my hair—I could feel strands of it sticking to my neck, slipping out of my bun. 'Nick, I'm going upstairs to tidy,' I said. 'I don't want a drink, but I'd love some coffee when I come down.' He brightened visibly.

'Of course,' he said, 'we'll have it in the lounge, then you needn't come back in here.'

Now that was thoughtful of him, for people were looking our way, they were staring at me, and I felt conspicuous. I lacked the cool of my erstwhile doctor assistant, who was talking to his girlfriend as though nothing had happened, although *she* looked suitably awed.

Up in the cloakroom I washed my face, applied new make-up, took down my hair, reknotted it, and instantly felt better. I had done the right things down there in the dining-room. I had helped save a life. It was true I'd had professional assistance, but even so, I hadn't done badly, I'd acted quickly. I sailed back downstairs feeling thankful, even grateful that I'd chosen medicine as a career.

I was very thirsty, and the first cup of coffee went down in a scalding rush. 'I needed that.' I poured myself another, beaming happily at Nick.

He didn't respond; he was looking disdainful as he sat there stirring his coffee. 'I don't know how you can possibly *do* that kind of thing,' he said jerkily, and just for a second I couldn't think what he meant. Then the penny dropped—of course, of *course*—he meant my kiss of life.

'If I hadn't done it,' I said quietly, for there were people sitting near, 'Mr Raunds would be on a morgue slab now, instead of in ICU being monitored, and given every care.'

'Someone else would have gone to his aid, if you hadn't flown off like that.'

'Maybe they would——' I began to feel cross '—but in a situation like that you don't hang back, you don't wait and see, you jump to it at once. As it happened I was helped, which was marvellous, it's always better with two.'

'I can't imagine a more revolting task.'

'That's unkind, and you know it is.'

Nick gulped at his coffee, making a drain sound as he swallowed. The last thing I wanted was to argue with him; I hated bandying words. And in a way I could sympathise with him, even understand his revulsion. I hadn't exactly enjoyed putting my mouth over Mr Raunds'. He had tasted of whisky and cigar smoke, and his beard had tickled my face in a kind of sickening intimacy, which in retrospect seemed worse than it had at the time, when all my concentration had been focused on his lungs.

So I had to be fair, 'But I know how you feel,' I added placatingly. He half smiled and put down his cup, he seemed to be deep in thought, then he reached for my hand—we were sitting on a couch—and gave it a little squeeze.

'Kate——' he cleared his throat '—there's something I want to say to you. It's really why I asked you to meet me for lunch. I wanted to get it straightened out before we go off to that medical party this evening.' I saw him moisten his lips.

'You sound very serious!'

'Don't joke, it's important.'

'Sorry, please go on.' But whatever was coming now? I wondered. I was very soon to find out.

'I want. . .' he began. 'I would like you to consider giving up work once we're married. In fact——' I felt his hand leave mine '—once you've finished your locum post, why not make the break then?'

I heard my own gasp, I stared at him, I tried to speak and failed. I was literally speechless for seconds, then words burst out of me. 'You *are* joking. . .you have to be joking. . .you can't possibly mean it! You can't mean it, not after all we said!'

'I'm not joking, and I do mean it. I would rather you gave up work.' His voice was quiet, mine was shrill in reply.

'But, Nick, I'm a doctor!'

'Well, exactly.' He was still speaking quietly. 'And that's the nub of it, isn't it? That's what it's all about. Your hours aren't. . .wouldn't be regular; I'd hardly ever see you. Our evenings and weekends would be broken into, there wouldn't be any peace. And when we went out, when we *managed* to go out, you would probably be on call, or there'd be some lurid incident, like just now.'

'Cardiac arrests aren't that common, thank God!'

'I think you know what I mean.' His tone was as sharp as mine now, which meant we were quarrelling.

'You've got it all wrong.' I strove to calm down. 'I'll make absolutely sure there'll be time for us to be together, and we discussed this, you know we did. I shall look for a partnership in a group practice, where regular days off, and weekends, will be arranged on a proper rota basis. We talked about this in Cheltenham, you can't have forgotten. You agreed to it on the spot, thought it would work out all right.'

'I'd have agreed to anything in Cheltenham.' He gave me the kind of smile which, coming just at that moment, made me want to hit him hard. He reached for my hand again, but I tugged it free, nearly losing my ring.

'It's taken me nine years to get where I am, Nick.' I was getting angry now. 'Once a doctor, always a doctor—I can't throw it all away!' It was the wrong tactic, the wrong line to take, I saw his face close up.

'I would have thought the status of marriage would be a fair exchange.'

'No,' I said baldly, and of course I should have explained a little more, but I didn't, I couldn't, I was too upset. I still couldn't believe that all this was happening. Nick was being so unfair.

'I shall have to be going.' He looked at his watch, and at me just as coldly. He had already paid the bill, and I'd got my coat lying there beside me. As we rose he helped me on with it, and, feeling his hand brush my neck for a second, all my anger fled. I wanted to turn to him, to be held by him, to beseech him to understand. I wanted a fair hearing, I wanted to be close to him again.

The uniformed doorman went to the kerb to hail a taxi for me, Nick waited with me till it came. 'If you think anything of me at all, Kate, you'll co-operate,' he whispered.

'You mean do as you say?'

'Not in all things, no.' He was looking huffy again, and a little injured, but there was no time to continue our argument now. The doorman had managed to flag down a taxi, I could see it doing its best to turn into the kerb, and he went forward to open its door.

'See you this evening,' was all I said as I got inside. Nick nodded and began to walk briskly away in the direction of Shaftesbury Avenue, weaving in and out of the crowds; he was very soon lost to sight.

It wasn't until I was at Liverpool Street, and sitting in the train, that I realised how upset I was, how dangerously close to tears. Nick and I had had words, we had disagreed on a very important issue. But it was his fault. . .it was his fault! How *could* he have said what he did? It wasn't as though we hadn't talked about my work when we'd first got engaged. We came to an agreement, made a plan, and now he was all second thoughts. 'Once a doctor, always a doctor,' I muttered under my breath, startling the girl sitting opposite me, who was eating an apple in a series of snaps, which set my teeth on edge.

The diesel train poured through the tunnels, through the inner and outer suburbs, then gathered speed, blaring its way towards the flat fields of East Anglia. Passengers were processing down the aisle, making for the buffet car. On the other side of the sleet-bespattered windows lights were springing up. It would be dark by the time we reached Seftonbridge, but I had left my car on the station forecourt. It wouldn't take long to get home.

Leaning back and closing my eyes, I let the events of the day roll through my mind like a length of film, starting with breakfast-time, soon after which I'd had a house call to make to a terminally ill patient. Morning surgery had come next, then a rush for the train, then London, then the Tube, and Bedford Square, the taxi to Rastners, and seeing the man who was so soon to help me, waiting at the foot of the stairs. I could still see him, very clearly indeed, for the mind's eye can be very sharp. I felt he was a caring type, and I wondered if he had a physician's post in a hospital, or was a GP like me. I didn't suppose I would ever find out, and the image of him faded as Nick's took precedence, and once more I could hear the back and forth of our conversation as we'd sat in the coffee lounge. Nick had been angry, he'd contained it well, but it had shown in every line of him; even his back view had shrieked it as he'd walked away from me.

He had always liked his own way, though, even when we were children. He had been the boy next door, my parents and his had owned adjoining houses in Park Road, Seftonbridge. Nick was three years older than me, he and my brother, Tom, had attended the same day school, and we had all gone around together. I can remember our tree-house even now, and the forbidden stretch of river where we were never, ever allowed to swim.

By the time I was seventeen, however, the threesome was coming apart. Nick and Tom were twenty, and were starting out in jobs—Tom joining Father in the family boatbuilding business, Nick becoming articled to

Alders and Fawn, Chartered Architects of Regent Street, W1.

As for me, I was set on becoming a doctor, and was working for my A levels, hoping to get in at one of the London teaching hospitals. I still saw Nick at weekends and was hopelessly in love with him, but there was nothing heavy between us, not in sexual terms. Most of it was fantasy on my part, for Nick never really saw me as other than Tom's kid sister, who could run like a hare, bowl a fast ball at cricket, and shin up a tree like a cat.

When I was eighteen I went up to London to train at the Walbrook hospital. There I met a galaxy of new people, and grew in confidence. I fell in and out of love several times, and felt only a passing pang when Nick married a young photographic model, and vanished from the scene.

The following year Tom married. He and his wife, Marian, decided to emigrate to New Zealand and start a business there. Father retired at about this time, and he and Mother went to live at Berwick-on-Tweed. I heard nothing of Nick till I turned twenty-four and was a registered doctor in my first month of GP traineeship with a practice in Cheltenham. I heard that he had divorced his wife, and was living back at Seftonbridge with his mother, his father having died.

I was sorry about this—well, naturally I was—it was Tom who gave me the news in one of his monthly letters, he was very cut up about it. 'Nick should have married you,' he said. 'What a funny old world it is.'

But I was finding the world very much to my liking, both professionally and socially. The next three years slipped away like lightning, and I was only four months off completing my traineeship, when Nick came to

Cheltenham to open a new branch for his firm and run it for a time. He got in touch with me, and it was like old times, like turning back the clock, only better than that, for Nick saw me as a woman and wanted me for his wife. I was quick to say yes, for marriage to Nick was a girlhood dream come true. We knew one another, we had grown up together, I had always wanted him.

I finished my traineeship, we were engaged at Christmas, and everything fell into place. Uncle John offered me the locum post, which I was only too glad to accept, because Nick was due back at London head office, and we didn't want to part. We made plans: we would look for a house, and marry during the summer. Nick would continue to commute to town, while I would hope to get a partnership in a group practice not too far from home. We agreed, though, that when we started a family—and we both wanted children—I would work part-time only, perhaps just do morning surgeries, or evening ones, or something along those lines.

But now all that, or the last part anyway, didn't suit Nick. Once again, all over again, I played out that scene in the coffee lounge. . .

And for the life of me, I couldn't think what to do.

CHAPTER TWO

AN HOUR later, back at the Larches, I garaged the car, and went straight through the surgery quarters, where I sat behind the desk, feeling headachy and miserable, but trying to overcome both.

Evening surgery was due to start in ten minutes and I had—I glanced at the list—ten or eleven patients to see. This was no time at all to dwell upon my own problems, and in any case I would be seeing Nick again later tonight; we could talk more rationally then, or I hoped we could. I slipped off my jacket and buttoned myself into my clean white coat and tried to stop worrying.

Aunt Laura, who always acted as receptionist after Doris Leigh had gone home, arrived with a tray of tea. 'I heard the car,' she said; 'we've got time to drink this before we start.' Flushed and cheerful, her grey hair clouding about her face, she set the tray down on the desk.

'Lovely, I can do with it.' I avoided her searching glance.

'You look tired, Kate, but then London always has that effect on me, too.' She moved to the window and drew down the blind, effectively shutting out the murky weather, which was just as bad here as it had been up in town. 'How was Nick?' She came back and sat down.

'Oh, just fine. We had lunch at Rastners.' I infused enthusiasm, even gaiety, into my voice, and smiled straight back at her.

'Nick has such good taste in everything.' She was looking at my ring—a diamond cluster—which Nick had slipped on to my finger last weekend. 'Now it's official,' he'd said, and kissed me. 'Now we can tell the world.'

Partly to keep Aunt Laura off the subject of Nick for the moment, I told her about Mr Raunds' collapse in Rastners' dining-room; how I'd given him the kiss of life, and been helped by an unknown doctor, who most likely, by the look of him, was a consultant of some kind.

'Good heavens, Kate, what an experience!' she cried. 'No wonder you look worn out! Darling, I'm sure you did a wonderful job.' Aunt Laura was one of those people who believed in praise and plenty of it. Aunt Laura was a love. 'Is the man all right,' she asked me, 'I mean the casualty?'

'I don't know,' I replied, 'but I'll find out, ring the Middlesex tomorrow. I shouldn't be surprised if the doctor who helped me will do so as well. He looked like a man who'd want to follow things through.'

'Don't you know who he was?' my aunt queried, gathering the tea-things up.

'No, I don't,' I said shortly, 'I've no idea, we didn't introduce ourselves. Well, there wasn't time, there was so much going on, and I'd left Nick just sitting, so I had to get back to him double-quick. You know what men are like.'

It was at this point that the waiting-room door opened and banged shut. Then a raucous cough, belonging to my first patient, Mrs Ainsworth, made Aunt Laura hurry out with the tray. It was five o'clock, time to start. After making sure that the medical notes tallied with the list, I opened the communicating door, and brought Mrs Ainsworth through. She had a chest infection, and puffed to a chair which was kept at the side of the desk. 'How have you been feeling?' I asked her, watching her drop her handbag of vast proportions down on the carpeted floor.

'Neither better nor worse,' she informed me gloomily, coughing to prove her words.

'Well, the antibiotic hasn't really had time to work yet,' I said, 'but if you'll take off your cardigan and blouse I'll listen to your chest again.'

Of course it wasn't just a case of cardigan and blouse, for Mrs Ainsworth had layers of clothes, but she cast them off very speedily, and I moved behind her chair. 'Will you cough for me, please, then take as deep a breath as you possibly can?'

She did both these things. She was very co-operative, and, apart from giving a jump when the cold disc of the stethoscope met her warm skin, she kept very still and very quiet, while I listened to the rattlings and musical murmurings going on in her lungs. 'Rhonchi and moist rales heard over lobes,' I wrote in her notes, and wrote her up for a linctus to ease her cough.

Next came a youth of thirteen with acne, his over-fussy mother answering all the questions I put to him, and asking so many herself that the boy lapsed into total silence. I tried to draw him out. 'It's a growing-up thing, Donald,' I said, 'this time next year you probably won't be bothered with it, but in the meantime don't squeeze the spots, just wash them frequently with mild soap and hot water, then rub in this lotion I'm prescribing for you; the chemist will make it up.'

They went out, the boy mumbling thanks, his mother looking aggrieved. 'Dr Spender would have put him on tablets,' she said, 'and cleared it up, once and for all.

What's the use of a lotion? Nothing like that ever works.'

'I don't like prescribing drugs unnecessarily,' I told her pleasantly. 'Persevere with the lotion, Donald, and come back and see me in a week.'

I saw three bronchitic ladies next, then a young girl with hypertension, two elderly gentlemen getting over flu, a child with a strep. throat, and finally a teacher from the primary school with a build-up of wax in her ears. I kept her sitting down for a time after I had syringed them. 'Just in case you turn dizzy,' I said. 'Occasionally people do. It's best to be sure, isn't it, rather than risking a fall?' She agreed that it was, and when she got up to go she thanked me effusively.

'All that awful crackling has gone, Doctor, and I can hear more clearly. I can hear your clock, and I couldn't before. I can't thank you enough. You've been so kind, and I've taken up so much of your time.'

'That's what I'm here for, Miss Mayhew.' I watched her lift her umbrella from the stand inside the waiting-room door and go off into the night.

There were swings and roundabouts in medicine, the same as in other jobs. Some patients were difficult to deal with, others co-operated; some were convinced that they knew all the answers, others listened to advice.

I yawned, not from boredom, but more to pretend that I wasn't feeling twitchy about seeing Nick again. It was always embarrassing seeing people after you'd had a row, but a face would have to be put on things, and quickly too, if my aunt and uncle weren't to suspect the true state of affairs. Oh, dear, I thought, how compli-cated life can be at times. Stripping off my surgery coat and locking the outside door, I went through into the living part of the house.

Uncle John was back from the last of his calls; he and Aunt Laura were talking in low tones as I entered the sitting-room. 'Ah, Katy, there you are!' Uncle was drinking tea, standing on the rug with his back to the fire. 'Finished at last, my dear?'

'Yes, all done.' I smiled at him. He was very like my father—big and blond and teddy-bear-like, gentle as they come.

'Your aunt has been telling me about your little adventure in town. What a good thing you were there on the spot. Nick must be proud of you.'

'I didn't do it all on my own, Uncle.' I ignored his last comment.

'No, so Laura said. How extraordinary that——'

'Kate, darling, Nick rang,' Aunt Laura cut in at this point. 'He asked me to tell you that he can't come this evening, he's feeling a little unwell. He said not to ring him back, he was going to lie down.'

'Oh!' I sat down on the arm of a chair, feeling as though I'd been slapped. 'Oh, dear, poor Nick,' I said quickly, just for appearance's sake. I didn't believe he was ill for a minute, not for a single second. He was avoiding the issue, keeping his head down, in more ways than one. He probably thought that if he gave me time in which to think, and stew, and fret, I would *give* in, agree to do as he wished. But nothing is ever solved by avoidance, it has to be gone into from every angle, and discussed without temper or tears.

'Perhaps it was something he ate at lunchtime.' Aunt Laura was looking anxious. 'Did you have the same, Kate. . .are you all right?'

'Yes, I'm perfectly all right, and we did have the

same.' I smiled strainedly back at her, and said, 'Poor Nick,' again, while wanting to strangle him.

'Well, I hope this doesn't mean *you* won't come, Kate,' Uncle John was saying. 'You ought not to miss this chance of meeting other doctors in the area. Besides, we want to show you off, don't we, dear?' He turned to Aunt Laura, who agreed with him, telling me there was plenty of hot water if I wanted a bath, and that we ought to be leaving in just about an hour.

'It's a good thing, isn't it,' I said, getting to my feet, 'that it's a buffet party and not a formal sit-down do, where a spare female might be a shocking embarrassment? Yes, of course I'm coming, I want to come, I've been looking forward to it.'

I made for the stairs, feeling fairly certain they had guessed there was something wrong. Aunt Laura had had her suspicions, I knew, when I'd walked in earlier on. Damn Nick, damn Nick! How could he do this to me? But, standing under the pelting shower, a feeling of disquiet needled through the mist of my anger, for supposing he really *was* ill? I dried quickly and went into the bedroom, wrapping myself in my robe. I stared at the phone on the bedside table and stretched out a hand to lift the receiver, then changed my mind and took it back again. Nick wasn't alone. Alma, his mother, would look after him if he was ill. She was fussy but sensible with it, and she would do all the right things. Anyway, all my vibes were insisting that he was no more ill than I was. We were both suffering from the same thing—ill temper after a row.

I hadn't dried myself properly, and I was chilly; I could see my goose-pimpled arms as I coiled up my hair at the dressing-table mirror, thinking all the time about Nick versus my career. What if I had to choose? If I didn't love him it would be easy, I muttered, I could tell him where to go—tell him to take a running jump, and do as I liked. I skewered the last pin into my knot, and sprayed perfume behind my ears. Loving a man shackled one, of course, in multifarious ways. Being one of a pair meant running in harness—harmoniously in harness—or life was a pain. I grimaced and turned from the glass.

My dress moved slinkily over my bust and hips. It was a jade-green jersey silk, long-sleeved and high-necked, with a fluted hemline and tiny gold buttons all down the centre back. With it I was wearing gold hoop earrings, my lipstick was 'Living Flame'. I have a large mouth and good teeth. Strawberry blondes who are neither plain nor beautiful, but a few shades in between, have to make the best of what they've got.

The party given by Dr Roseveare and his wife was an annual event. Their house was on the other side of Seftonbridge on the borders of Elverton. I knew that most of the guests would be general practitioners, but there would also be doctors from the big general hospital just off Princes Parade. 'I especially want you to meet James Masefield,' Uncle John remarked, driving slowly and carefully, as he always did, down St Andrew's Street out to Grange Road. 'He runs a single-handed practice in Theodore Road, and is the GP I cover for, now and again, to give him a free weekend. He wants to be off tomorrow and Sunday, and as this is my golfing weekend I've told him that you'll stand in for him; I know Rose would have done. What we do is get Telecom to divert his calls direct to the Larches. This needn't stop you going out with Nick, so long as Laura knows where to reach you, should anything come through.'

'You might have asked Kate first, dear,' Aunt Laura remonstrated. Sometimes she was apt to forget that Uncle was my boss.

'Oh, it's perfectly all right,' I said quickly. 'Nick and I haven't made any plans.'

'That's my girl.' Uncle sounded pleased. 'You'll like James, I'm sure. He's very hard-working, a dedicated type, but he's got far too much on his plate. He's a widower, so has no one close to take the strain at home.'

Somehow or other from all this I expected an elderly doctor. It was therefore a shock when, in the Roseveares' sitting-room some ten minutes later, I saw, walking towards us, a tall, dark man in his middle thirties—an eye-catching, striking man, who would stand out in any company. He was looking astonished, more than that—astounded—and I dare say I was too, for James Masefield—Dr James Masefield—was my partner in the restaurant, the man who had helped me resuscitate Mr Raunds.

Uncle John, who had whispered, 'Kate, this is James,' as soon as he'd seen him coming, introduced me formally, all but pushing me on to my toes. 'Meet my niece, Kate Chalmers, James, who, as I told you, is my locum while Rose Spender is adapting to motherhood.'

'Good evening, Kate,' James Masefield said gravely, and for the second time that day his warm hand curled about mine, causing such a disturbance all the way up my arm that I felt it was living a life of its own. He didn't seem worried about explanations, but I very quickly made them.

'We've already met.' I turned to Uncle. 'Dr Masefield is the doctor I told you about, who helped me in the restaurant, when that man collapsed.' My words came out jerkily in a series of shots. I was still feeling knocked for six.

'We made a good team,' James Masefield said, and as I drew my hand from his I heard Uncle and Aunt going on and on about what a small world it was, and what a coincidence, and all the rest of it. 'And it's especially extraordinary, isn't it, James,' Uncle said excitedly, 'for you don't go to town all that often, do you, being rushed off your feet as you are?'

James Masefield smiled and agreed with him. 'That's perfectly true, I don't, but I was lunching my young sister, who's at London University. It's her birthday today, her twenty-first, so celebrations were in order, and brothers have to put themselves out.'

'Oh, certainly they do,' Aunt Laura agreed, while I slowly digested the fact that the red-haired girl hadn't been quite what I thought.

After a little more chat, and once my uncle and aunt had wandered off, James Masefield suggested that we fetched some food and sat down together. Getting my breath back, I was only too glad to agree.

'Don't the patients find it a little confusing with two Dr Chalmerses in the practice?' he asked a few minutes later when, with well-filled plates, we sat down at the side of the room to eat.

'I'm usually known as Dr Kate,' I said, trying my level best to spear a difficult piece of salad and get it into my mouth.

'Dr Kate has a very nice ring to it.'

'Mm.' I returned his smile. I would have been hard put to it not to, for it was an infectious kind of smile, giving full rein to his humorous mouth, crinkling up his eyes and looking, as well as devastating, interested and kind. It was the kindness that grabbed me; it warmed me through, made me feel I mattered. He must, I thought, still wrestling with my lettuce, be a fantastic doctor. I wasn't in the least surprised he was over-worked. And neither was I surprised when he told me he'd already telephoned the Middlesex hospital about Mr Raunds.

'He's breathing for himself, his condition is stable, and he'll probably be transferred from Intensive Care to the cardiac ward in a day or two,' he said.

'We did a good job.'

'You especially. You were there in double-quick time, and, as we both know, time is of the essence—is of the utmost importance when someone's bellows have packed up.'

'Poor man, I'm glad he's recovering.'

'He's a classic example, I think, of a man who eats well but not wisely, and doesn't take enough exercise. But that sounds like preaching, which my young sister is always accusing me of!' He smiled ruefully, then rather differently, and my heart began to race. 'Let's forget Mr Raunds, shall we, and talk about other things, like you and your job. How are you enjoying your *locum tenens* post?'

'Very much,' I enthused, 'in fact I love it, even after only a week.'

'And you've been kind enough to agree to stand in for me this weekend.' He clutched his plate and held on grimly as someone passed our knees.

'I have, and I'm pleased to do it,' I tried not to sound too eager, 'so if there is anything special I ought to know about——'

'I don't think there is,' he interrupted, 'but if you could spare the time to come to my house early tomorrow I could show you where everything is, and give you the keys.'

'Of course.' I swallowed and nearly choked. 'Will half-eight be all right?'

'Perfect,' he said, wincing a little as someone trod on his foot. The room was too crowded, and people milled about us; we were all but cocooned in legs.

We ate in silence for a few minutes, and I took to wondering about his love-life, for he had to have one, looking as he did. 'Uncle was telling me how busy you are,' I ventured carefully. 'It must be difficult for you to get time off, and no one can work without breaks.'

'That's true, of course.' He laid down his fork and swivelled his legs towards me. 'When I first came here, five years ago, I had a workable list, but since then there has been a good deal of house-building going on. Families have moved into the area, and I'm getting to the stage when I'll have to take in a partner, or I'll never be able to cope. I'm thinking along the lines of a woman GP with family commitments who might want to work part-time, say twenty hours per week.'

'I'm sure that would suit quite a few married doctors.' I tried to quell my excitement. Would Nick agree. . . would he agree to my working part-time? Twenty hours per week would mean I could have masses of time at home. But he didn't really want me to work at *all*, he hated the thought of it. And now my excitement was turning to revolt.

'I had in mind,' James was saying, and he was staring at me hard, 'someone who could do, say, morning surgeries, and a share of house-calls, but no night calls, and only one weekend in four.'

'I see.' Hope reared again, and I took a sip from my glass.

'And I see that you're engaged to be married.' His eyes were on my ring. 'Do you intend to marry before you've finished your locum post?'

'No, after,' I told him, 'then I *had* planned to look for a partnership—full-time, of course, then part-time when we. . .when I started a family.'

'But you're reconsidering that, are you?' He didn't miss very much. Right at that moment I had the feeling that he didn't miss a thing, that he could identify all my thought processes, and knew I was interested in the possibility of joining his practice. I had the grace to blush. 'I take it,' he added, 'that your fiancé is the man you were lunching with today?'

'Yes, that was Nick, and I'm afraid,' I said, as calmly as I could, 'that he isn't quite certain how he feels about me working. It's something we have to discuss. . .he's only thinking of me, of course.' I added that out of loyalty, but knew it wasn't true. It was a flat lie, and I dare say James Masefield knew it too.

'Perhaps he doesn't want you to be too committed.' And now *he* was being careful, his tone was level, and his eyes looked straight into mine.

'That's what it is.' I saw him nod.

'May I ask where you plan to live?'

'Oh, in this area,' I answered readily, as he stacked my plate with his. 'We're looking for a house now, which is very exciting, of course. Nick is an architect, with a post in London; he lives with his mother at present. We've known one another on and off since childhood, he was my brother's friend. Tom married a New Zealand girl and went to live out there.' I was deliberately swerving the talk a little. I felt it was best to keep off the subject of future working until I had talked with Nick.

'I expect you miss your brother.' James took the hint, and what he said was right on target, for sometimes I felt bereft without Tom. We had always got on well.

'I miss him terribly,' I said quietly, 'and so do my parents. They moved up to Berwick-on-Tweed soon after he emigrated. Mother is an Edinburgh Scot, so not far from her roots. Father is retired, but keeps busy with their garden, which is the size of two fields. Mother breeds Border terriers, and whenever I go there the care of the dogs is always turned over to me.'

James laughed. 'The difference between a doctor and a vet not being thought too vast.'

'Evidently not,' I agreed, and as I smiled back at him I felt that he understood many things. He was an understanding man, not the type to scoff at, or denigrate, other people's careers. I hoped he might tell me more about himself, and perhaps he would have done, but someone was bellowing for silence, so that a little speech of thanks could be made to the Roseveares for laying on such a splendid party for the tenth year running, each year better than the last.

After that Uncle John appeared and dragged me off to meet so many doctors and social workers and paramedics that I forgot their names almost as soon as I'd shaken hands with them. One of them clung, and wouldn't be dislodged—a registrar from the hospital— who told me that my hair was the colour of autumn leaves, while my eyes were the green of Scottish lochs.

'What lovely compliments,' I said politely, looking round for James. He had been joined by a girl in black, with shoulder-length fair hair. People were walking and criss-crossing in front of me, so I couldn't see them well. Aunt Laura was agitating to go, so very soon after that we said goodbye to our hosts and made our way out to the car.

'How did you get on with James?' asked Uncle, grappling with his seatbelt. It was still sleeting, and the car felt very cold.

'Oh, I liked him,' I said, 'and I told him it was OK for the weekend.'

'That business in town was really extraordinary—I mean for it to be James, but it must have got the two of you off to a flying start.' As we turned out of the drive we nearly hit a passing cyclist who was tearing along without lights. 'Stupid young fool!' Uncle John breathed fire, Aunt Laura clicked with her tongue.

'How did Dr Masefield's wife die? Was it in an accident? She must have been very young,' I added, thankful for the warmth from the car's heater that was filtering through to the back.

'She *was* young, about your age, died in a plane crash, poor girl. She was Swiss by birth, and was flying out to Lausanne to visit her folk. The plane came down over the Alps, there were no survivors. You probably remember reading about it. . .it was about three years ago.'

'Oh, how dreadful,' I said, and meant it. 'What a terrible shock for him.'

'Some people say he has never got over it——' Aunt Laura turned her head to speak to me over her shoulder '—but he puts a good face on things, and of course he's got Eloise.'

'Is she the fair girl who was with him just now?' I asked, feeling sure she was.

'No, Eloise is his little daughter.' Uncle John braked at the lights. 'She'd have been about four when her mother was killed. James is devoted to her.'

'The fair girl is Helen Clifford,' Aunt Laura explained. 'She's a dental surgeon with Gregson and Partners, they have a surgery in Bateman Street. She and James are friendly—some people say more than that.'

'Now Laura, no gossiping,' Uncle said testily.

'She's an attractive girl, and he's a man. It's time he married again. Patients expect their GP to be married, it makes them feel comfortable.'

Uncle John said something that sounded like, 'Pooh,' changing gear as the lights turned to green.

'He must have help at home, surely?' I enquired from the back.

'Oh, he does,' replied Uncle, 'first-class help in the shape of a living-in housekeeper, Mrs Shinway, who takes full charge of the child. Her husband, Bob, lives in as well, and helps in the garden, although his real full-time job is a porter at the General. The arrangement seems to work well.'

'I see,' I said, clearing the window and looking out as we crossed Garrods Bridge with its old-fashioned lamps casting a glow on the water. We were nearly home, only yards to go now and Nick loomed large in my mind. Was he all right. . .was he really all right, or was he ill and sickening for something? I could have misjudged him, he could be dangerously ill and in need of attention. Alma might not realise. A lunge of anxiety made me move to the edge of my seat. I wouldn't be able to rest easy, I knew, until I had found out. I had to know if he was all right, nothing and no one else mattered, not even our quarrel. How stupid to quarrel; the handle of the door was ice in my palm as I levered it down and stepped out into our drive.

In the privacy of my bedroom I lifted the receiver,

dialled with shaking fingers and immediately got that mournful little sound which meant the line was engaged. I waited, then tried again; the same thing happened. I waited a little longer next time, walking round the room, picking things up and putting them down, looking at my watch. I tried again; it was still engaged, then I thought I knew what had happened. Nick had got his receiver off, he had really meant what he said. He didn't want to be disturbed, not by anyone, especially by me, and that hooting sound was like an awful reproach. But was he ill? How could I find out? I could go to him, motor over. I was halfway to the door when the phone shrilled, I turned back and snatched it up, nearly falling across the bed in my haste, relieved beyond measure to hear Nick's quick, light voice sifting into my ear.

'Hello, Kate. I rather thought you might be back home now.'

'Oh, Nick. . .' I was pretty near speechless. 'How are you, are you all right? I've been trying to ring you, but you were engaged.'

'I've had the receiver off, my head's been bad, but I'm feeling better now. Things got out of hand at lunchtime, didn't they? I didn't mean to upset you.' He was apologising, or as good as, which was good enough for me.

'Oh, Nick, it's all right, I'm sorry, I've been worried ever since!' I was quick to leap in with my own apology, for all I wanted was to heal the breach before it widened and left us both adrift.

'Perhaps,' he said, and I got the feeling he was choosing his words with care, 'we could come to some sort of compromise, about your work, I mean.'

'What kind of a compromise?' I was wary.

'Well, perhaps you could do short hours—part-time—right from the start. That way I could be sure of your company in the evenings and at weekends.'

'Why, yes.' I was almost too excited to say anything for a minute, for this was precisely what I'd had in mind ever since James Masefield had told me he would soon be looking for a part-time partner. I had the nous, though, not to mention this, for now wasn't the time. And neither was it the time to mention who James *was*—to bring all that up now would be asking for trouble, I felt. I would tell him, but not now, so all I said was, 'I'll certainly settle for part-time, Nick. I think that could work out quite well.'

'Kate, I do love you, you know,' came after a breathy sigh.

'And I love you, and I loathe quarrelling.' Both these things were true. I began to relax, to feel very much better. I'd been silly to worry so much. 'You never have much time to spare at lunchtime, and that makes for strain,' I said. 'We'd better meet locally in future.'

'Yes, like tomorrow,' he was quick to reply. 'Where shall we go? You're not on call, I hope.'

'Well, actually, yes.' I played this one carefully, for I had two things on in the morning—my visit to James Masefield's surgery and then, back at the Larches, I had a patient coming for a check-up for life insurance. 'I'm standing in for Uncle John and for another GP over the weekend,' I explained, 'but there shouldn't be anything much happening—fingers crossed, of course. We could go out in the evening, so long as we don't go too far away.'

'How about dinner at the White Swan?' This came out after a pause.

'Terrific, but how extravagant!'

'I'll pick you up at seven.'

'Nick,' I said, and once more I felt I was treading on delicate ground, 'perhaps it would be better if I picked *you* up. I ought to have my own car, just in case I get called away—not that I think that's likely to happen, but best to be prepared.'

'I see, I take your point.' There was a pause and then he laughed. 'And I agree on condition that you promise to see me safely home.'

'Hand on heart!' I laughed back, then wondered why I felt a sudden chill, like a drenching wind, then decided it was the draught from the partly open window. I closed it when Nick had rung off.

CHAPTER THREE

A PALE sun gleamed on the nose of the Renault, as I drove out to Theodore Road early next morning, and drew up in front of a red-brick Victorian house that had James's name engraved on a brass plate just to the right of the gate.

It was he who opened the door to me, casually dressed in a dark blazer and smooth light trousers, and once again I had the sensation that my heart was beating a Highland fling in my chest as he smiled at me and invited me inside.

'You're very punctual.' He was taller than me by about half a head, so he didn't have very far to look down to scrutinise my face, which was what he appeared to be doing, as though he was making sure that it really was me and not my look-alike standing in a state of entrancement in his hall.

'I've got a patient coming at half-nine,' I said, and somehow or other this true remark, which had come out on a wash of embarrassment, sounded as though I'd scarcely got time to come out all this way, and was doing him a favour, so would he please hurry up? I was sure this was how he took it too, for he opened a door on our left and ushered me into a bay-windowed room, which was clearly his surgery. He crossed to the filing cabinets.

'I'll give you the keys to these.' He opened a drawer in his leather-topped desk, bending his head and craning his neck to see right to the back. This gave me a

36

clear chance to study him and I made the most of it, not moving any closer, but still not missing much. His hair was thick and so dark a brown it was very nearly black—the springy, spruce short kind, that would curl if given a chance. His brows were jet black. I looked away quickly as he found the keys and stood up. 'I'm grateful to you for doing this, Kate.' The drawer closed with a click. 'It gives me a chance to see my parents in Sussex, something I can't often do.'

You have only to ask, were the words in my head, but I didn't give them voice, I rejected them in favour of the more dignified, 'That's perfectly all right.' I could feel the colour warming my face as he handed me the keys. I was looking at him and not at them, so perhaps it wasn't surprising that they dropped from my fingers and plopped down on my shoe. I bent to pick them up, so did he, at the self-same moment. . .and we cracked heads. . .and the room flashed and split into strings of coloured lights. They curved round and spun, like a wheel, I heard James's startled grunt, then felt his hands beneath my elbows, raising me, lifting me up.

'Kate. . . Kate, I'm so sorry!' His breath was tickling my face.

'So am I,' I said with feeling, grinning through tears of pain, but the wheels and whorls of light had stopped turning, I could just see him, I could just see James, near and clear, and what more could a woman ask? He was touching my forehead, fingertips gentle as they moved across my brow.

'It was such an unequal contest.' The corners of his mouth twitched upwards a little. 'I've a thicker head than yours.'

'Let's just say heavier,' I said, coming out of my

trance. I moved back deliberately, and he let go of my arms.

'Are you all right?'

'Absolutely,' I said, pocketing the keys. 'It takes more than a cracked skull to floor me!' I could still feel it, of course, but even more strongly I could feel another sensation altogether—a tingling where his fingers had been, a delicious sensation that had nothing whatever to do with pain. 'I must go,' I said stiffly, and turned to the door, just as it opened wide and a little girl in a red coat and hood rushed forward to James.

'Hello, poppet, all ready, I see,' he said, turning her round, holding her against his legs to face me. 'Meet my daughter, Eloise. Lou, this is Dr Kate, who is looking after our patients while we're at Lewes. Isn't that kind of her?'

'Yes.' She looked at me doubtfully, as I squatted down to her height.

'You're going to see your grandparents, I hear. That'll be lovely, won't it?'

She nodded. She had her father's blue eyes and thick dark hair—what I could see of it—thrusting out in curls beneath her hood. 'I want Rollo to come,' she told me, looking disconsolate, 'but Daddy and Helen don't want him, because he's sick in the car.' She looked round at her father, who pulled a face at her.

'Sorry, darling, but that's not very nice for him, or for us. If you asked him I'm quite sure he'd tell you that he'd rather be left at home. Mrs Shinway will look after him and take him for his walks. Rollo is our Labrador,' he explained, as Eloise ran to the window and peered through the net curtain, pressing it close to the pane.

'Helen's here.' She let go of the curtain. 'Are we going in her car or ours?'

I heard him say, 'Ours,' heard a car door slam, followed by the crunching of feet on gravel, then the slipping sound of them coming up the steps.

'I must go,' I said, for the second time, moving out into the hall. James followed me, but I knew it was inevitable that I would have to meet Helen Clifford, the fair girl from the party, the dentist from Bateman Street, who was at the door now with her finger on the bell. Eloise reached up and opened the door, and there she was, pale hair just clearing the shoulders of her blue tweed suit. She was carrying a grip, which she put down to shake hands with me. Her hand felt tiny and boneless, her blue eyes matched her suit.

'I noticed you at the party last night.' She smiled, showing small, even teeth. 'James told me who you were; I knew everyone else, of course.'

'It was crowded, wasn't it?' I felt lamp-post-tall against her five foot nothing. 'It was difficult to circulate.'

'Oh, I do agree. I was late coming. It was all I could do to squeeze my way over to James, let alone move around.' Her eyes had a kind of flashing brilliance that disconcerted me. 'It's so good of you,' she went on, 'to relieve James this weekend. Let's hope you won't be bothered with too many tiresome calls.'

'I don't think that's very likely,' James said evenly, looking round as a large cream dog appeared from the back regions, dragging behind him a sturdy little woman in a flowered overall. Her glasses—the rimless kind—were slipping down her nose. Once again, I could guess who she was, and once again introductions got under way. Mrs Shinway and I shook hands.

After that, and saying goodbye to them all, I managed to make my exit, James coming down the steps and standing on the gravel as I drove off. Glancing in the mirror, I was just in time to see the blue-eyed Helen Clifford join him and link her arm in his. There was something proprietorial about the gesture. How close were they? I wondered. Perhaps they intended to marry, perhaps this weekend visit to James's parents was to consolidate wedding plans. She didn't wear an engagement ring, still that didn't necessarily mean they *weren't* engaged. It had been some weeks before Nick and I chose my ring. I touched it with the ball of my thumb, rather expecting, I think, that Nick, like the Genie of the Lamp, would appear before my eyes. I was seeing him tonight, there'd be no more harsh words, we'd talk things out properly. We were right for one another, we always had been, always would be, too. That brief, *very* brief moment, when James's face had been close, when his long, sensitive fingers had traced magic across my brow, must be forgotten, and the sooner the better. With a great effort of will I began to think about Mrs Dahl, my nine-thirty patient, who was most likely sitting in the waiting-room right at this moment, wondering when Dr Kate was going to show.

'She's here!' Aunt Laura hissed, as soon as I walked in. And she was, too, I could see her shadow through the glass-panelled door as I thrust my arms into my white coat and sat down at the desk. The insurance company's questionnaire was open on the blotter, my stethoscope and sphygmomanometer were there, ophthalmoscope and wipes, there was a fresh strip of sheeting on the examination couch, and a towelling dressing-gown, ready for slipping on. Aunt Laura had been doing her stuff again; everything was in order. I got to my feet and called Mrs Ivy Dahl through.

In she came in an ocelot coat, with the collar turned up all round. I gave her the dressing-gown, and asked her to strip, pulling the curtains round the couch to give her privacy. 'Shout when you're ready,' I said, 'and don't rush, there's plenty of time.'

The examination followed its normal course. I took a blood specimen, labelled the urine sample she'd produced, asked about hobbies and exercise. She dressed while I filled in details on the form. I had nearly finished when she swished back the curtains and came to sit at the desk.

'Have you found anything? Am I all right?' she asked, and I put down my pen. Patients who came in for routine check-ups always asked that. It was natural enough, goodness knows; I'd have done the same. It was the ones with specific symptoms who were often too scared to enquire.

'We'll have to wait for the laboratory reports on your specimens,' I said, 'but from my examination this morning you seem to be in good health. Your blood pressure is a shade higher than I'd like to see it, but that could be due to nervousness coming here, of course. You could do with losing a little weight, you're half a stone too heavy, which isn't much, but, as you probably know, once weight begins to creep up, it has a habit of following that pattern. Cut down on fats and sugar, if you can, and take a little more exercise. Walk, instead of taking a bus, for instance, and swimming is excellent.'

'Thank you, Doctor.' She peered at me over the rim of her collar, her bleached hair that had got pushed up as she lay on the couch rising in a cone at the back of her head. 'Are you going to be here always now?' she asked, as I let her out.

'No, only until mid-May, then Dr Spender will be back.'

'Are you Dr Chalmers's daughter?'

'No, I'm his niece.'

'Oh, I see,' she said, and off she went, high heels clacking. There was nothing wrong with her curiosity, I could have given her full marks for that. I saw the bus halt at the end of the road and guessed she was getting on it. So much for the extra exercise, and quite likely, I thought, she'd get off at McDonalds and treat herself to a quarter-pounder, to tide her over till lunchtime. Some people wouldn't be helped.

I looked at the clock; it was nearly ten-thirty. No doubt James, and Eloise, and the flawless Helen, would be well on their way southwards into Sussex. Eloise was very like her father, she had his sensitive mouth—long with mobile corners. She'd been upset about the dog. Surely they could have taken it with them, given it a Marzine or Avomine, to stop it being ill. Oh, well, it was none of my business. With a great effort of will I banished all thoughts of the family party heading for Lewes. Instead I ate a belated breakfast, and prepared for the house call I had promised to do for Uncle John, to a bed-ridden patient who needed a weekly injection of Vitamin B.

Back home again I helped Aunt Laura with the chores. We had a snack lunch at two o'clock, then spent the afternoon clearing out the garden shed, well wrapped up in thick coats and head-scarves, for the sun had spent itself. I was chilly from nerves, on edge all the time, in case the phone should ring. This was the first time I had covered for anyone other than Uncle

John, and now I had the temporary care of both his patients and James's. Admittedly nothing appeared to be happening, but one never knew when it might. I was suffering from the new broom syndrome; most doctors have it at first.

Although I wanted to see Nick, I couldn't help wishing that he were coming here to the Larches, and that we weren't going out. When I mentioned this to Aunt Laura she said we were perfectly welcome to stay in if we wanted to, but was that fair to Nick, who was all for taking me out and giving me a treat? 'After all, I know where you'll be,' she went on, 'and I can ring you at the White Swan in the twinkling of an eye, should anything happen. Kate, love, I do know how you feel, but if you take your job too seriously you'll end up being a bore, *and* with an ulcer before you're thirty. Go out and enjoy yourself.'

So I went, driving the mile and a half across town to Park Road. When I got there Nick was still upstairs getting ready. His mother, Alma Carrington, was beating up eggs in the kitchen. 'With Nick out of the way I can eat what I fancy,' she laughed. 'He doesn't like omelettes.' She set down the basin and gave me a quick hug. She was pleased about our engagement. 'It should have been you the first time,' she had said just over a month ago, when we'd rung her from Cheltenham. 'Do let me see your dress,' she said now, making me take off my coat. It wasn't a dress, it was a skirt and blouse— the skirt long and black, the blouse belted over it, white with enormous sleeves. My necklace was jet, and so were my earrings; my hair was piled on top. Alma enthused and told me I looked the picture of elegance.

'I hope I match up,' said a voice from the doorway, and Nick walked in, clad, as I was, in black and white, his well-cut dinner-jacket accentuating his fairness. He looked great, and I told him so.

'All the same, you'd better have a coat of some sort, it's bitterly cold and rain is forecast,' said Alma, flying up the stairs.

'You'd think I was ten years old.' A look of annoyance crossed Nick's face, but he took the light raincoat his mother came back with, and thrust his arms into the sleeves. 'I can't wait to get settled into our own home,' he said, as we got in the car. Then he kissed me before I could make any comment. 'I've missed you very much.'

'We saw one another yesterday.' I returned his kiss in full measure.

'Yes, I know we did, but we quarrelled, which made the in-between time worrying.'

'Oh, Nick!' I knew what he meant exactly; this was one of our close times. We kissed again, then sat back to fasten our belts.

The sharp smell of his aftershave eddied about my head. He was such a clean man, he always looked clean. I had never seen him other than bandbox-neat; he said it went with his job. I felt, though, that it was part and parcel of the person he was, for even as a boy he had never got scruffy and dirty like Tom and me. But this evening we matched, we both looked good, and a few minutes later, as we entered the beamed dining-room of the White Swan Hotel, I felt settled and happy. Things were going to be all right.

'I'm glad you're only going to work part-time once we're married,' he said, over the soup course, bringing out the remark with a certain amount of diffidence, keeping his eyes on his plate.

'Part-time seems fair to both of us, and I'm happy to

settle on that,' I said carefully, wishing he would look me in the face. 'Woman doctors often do part-time hours *and* get partnerships.'

'So you do still want a partnership?'

'Well, frankly, yes,' I said. 'I don't want a string of locum posts, I want to feel attached.'

'I see.' He still wasn't looking at me, and after his spoon had gone up and down three times more I broke the news that the GP I was standing in for this weekend was James Masefield, the one who had helped me in town.

'How did *that* come about?' He did look at me then, but after I'd explained he appeared to lose interest, to be thinking of something else. I felt both relieved and deflated—more of the latter, I think. There was no doubt about it, you just never knew with men.

We seemed stuck for conversation, then, quite suddenly, totally without warning, Nick started to tell me about his marriage, which was the very last thing I expected just at that moment. 'My marriage to Lorraine failed because of her work,' he said thickly. 'Her hours were eccentric, to say the least; she was always travelling around. There was never any time to build a relationship, to strengthen what. . .little we had. We were both young, too young.' His face became suffused. 'I don't particularly like talking about it, but I'm doing so because it may help you to understand my feelings, to understand why at rock bottom I would rather you didn't work at all. I would rather you made *me* your career, but, having said all that, I have to respect your feelings in the matter, so we'll settle for part-time.'

'It'll be all right, Nick, I promise you.' I was suddenly conscience-stricken. Was I being fair to him? Was I being selfish? Should I be saying, 'I'll give up everything, just to be your wife'? Perhaps I should, but I knew I couldn't. All I could manage was, 'So, please, please, don't worry, our marriage will always come first.'

'That's another promise, is it?' His lip curled a little.

'It's the same one. I'll do everything in my power to make you happy.'

The waiter removed our plates at that point, creating a small diversion, which was welcome, for Nick's expression was tight. 'But you intend to be Dr Kate for the next thirty years,' he challenged.

'Dr Carrington, surely?' I was shocked at his tone.

'*Mrs* Carrington, so far as I'm concerned,' he said, and I swallowed hard on that.

'Oh, well, who cares about titles?' I managed to laugh, and we started to eat the roast lamb and vegetables that had been set in front of us. But we ate in a silence that was loaded, thick and heavy like fog. I racked my brains for something to say that would lighten the atmosphere. I could understand Nick's reservations only too well. He wanted to be married and to marry me, but it was going to take a long time . . .a very long time before I could convince him that my career wouldn't get in the way. The failure of his marriage to Lorraine had left a searing scar and a rooted prejudice against working wives, which might take years to dispel. It was going to be up to me to see that he got a continuing dose of TLC.

'We ought to start looking at houses, you know. Time is getting on,' he said, as we progressed to cheese and biscuits; neither of us liked sweet things.

'We certainly ought.' Now, this was better. Nick was smiling again. I smiled back. Oh, how good it would be, how lovely to have our own house, not too far from the river, and with a garden we could sit in. We were deep in a conversation about the kind of plants we would grow when over Nick's shoulder I saw the head waiter bearing down on us. He was coming for me, I knew he was, he was looking straight at me. Caught in the laser beam of his stare, I was already on my feet when he halted and said,

'Dr Chalmers, you're wanted on the phone. I would bring it in here, but I thought you would prefer to have privacy.' He took off his glasses, which had steamed up, and rubbed them on his front.

'Yes, I would, but where. . .?' I was edging out.

'In my office, please follow me.'

'I'll come back and tell you what's happening, if anything,' I said quickly to Nick, who was half sitting, half standing, and looking incredulous.

Oh, God, I thought, what awful timing, what diabolical luck. But once in the waiter's little office, listening to Aunt Laura's voice, I didn't think of anything but the message that was being relayed. A child of twelve was very ill. 'Acute abdomen, Kate, she's been ill since breakfast-time, so her mother, Mrs Staves, said. She's one of James Masefield's patients. I said you'd be there in ten minutes. Lenham Road, as you probably remember, is the third turning past the church, not far from the Swan, which is lucky.'

'Thanks, Aunt, I'm on my way.' I put down the phone, then raced back into the dining-room to Nick. 'Wait here for me, Nick, finish your meal. I don't suppose I'll be long, but don't go—wait here,' I picked up my evening bag.

'Is it an emergency?'

'Sounds like it.'

'OK, then, I'll hang on.' He didn't look pleased, but

there was nothing I could do to smooth him over just then. I rushed to the cloakroom to get my coat, then out to the car. My medical bag was on the back seat, I was off and away to Lenham Road, driving through rain that misted my side-windows up. Number eight was at the far end. Well, it would be, wouldn't it? But I found it without difficulty—a semi-detached house with a timber gable. I drew up at the gate.

Every window was lit, so was the porch, and the front door opened wide to stream out more light as I hurried up the path. A woman of about my own age came out and pulled me inside. 'The leaping pain has stopped now, Doctor, but she looks so dreadfully ill. My husband said I should have called you earlier, he's only just got in.' Mr Staves was coming down the stairs—a bald-headed little man, looking much older than his wife.

'What's your daughter's name?' I asked them, taking off my coat, feeling extremely unprofessional in my evening skirt and blouse.

'Jenny,' Mrs Staves said brokenly, leading the way upstairs. Mr Staves followed, enquiring where Dr Masefield was.

'He's away this weekend. I'm covering for him.' Mr Staves probably thought I looked about as much like a doctor as one of the Geisha girls. One look at his daughter, however, told me she was very ill indeed. Her face was grey with a malar flush, her eyes were sunken and ringed, and she was breathing quickly and shallowly, with a queer little jerking hisp.

'I'm sorry you're having such a rough time, Jenny.' I took her temperature and pulse, found the first to be high, and the second rapid; then examined her abdomen, noting how she was lying with her arms on the pillow beside her head. 'I'd like her in hospital,' I told the parents, out on the landing. 'She has an acutely inflamed appendix and it might have perforated.'

'I ought to have called you sooner, shouldn't I. . .? I ought to have called you sooner!' Mrs Staves clutched her husband, whose face went nearly as grey as his little girl's.

'May I use your phone to make the arrangements and call an ambulance?' I asked.

Mrs Staves nodded. 'Of course, go ahead. The phone is in the hall.'

'And would you like me to explain to Jenny?' I glanced at the bedroom door.

'No, I will.' Again it was Mr Staves who replied. 'She's a sensible girl, she won't make any fuss.'

'Perhaps. . .' I looked at the mother '. . .you would pack a bag for her, just her nightdress and toilet things, slippers and dressing-gown. Leave her in bed till the ambulance comes, but prop her up in a sitting position. It's important she shouldn't lie flat.'

I think they were glad of something to do, while I was glad to be left alone to telephone, and make the admittance arrangements. Within half an hour Jenny was on her way to the General Hospital, her parents following in their car.

Standing in the slanting rain in front of their locked-up house, I watched them go, then walked down the path to my car. With swift surgical intervention and modern drug therapy, Jenny Staves would most likely pull through, but peritonitis was a serious illness, and a painful condition to have. I'll ring through early tomorrow and find out how she is, I thought, as I drew away from the kerb.

I passed the church, noting the time—exactly nine p.m. Nick would have had to kick his heels in the hotel for nearly an hour. Still, it couldn't be helped, and I'd soon be there. I turned into Hobson's Lane, which was a steeply cambered secondary road, leading to the White Swan.

The lights were less garish here, but fully adequate. I could see a stationary car in the distance, very carelessly parked. Its chassis was sticking out into the road. Who on earth would park like that? I peered through the wipered arc of my windscreen, then slammed on my brakes as my lights picked out the figure of a girl racing towards me, waving her arms; she was clearly very distressed.

I pulled into the side; the girl reached me, and tugged open the door, sobbing wildly. 'Oh, please can you come? I've knocked someone down. . .a man. . . I think he's dead! He stepped straight out in front of me . . .it wasn't my fault! I had no chance to stop. . . I couldn't believe. . .'

'All right, all right. . . I'll come, calm down! I'm a doctor.' I reached for my case. 'Have you called an ambulance?'

'No, it's only just happened. . . I haven't. . .'

'Then do so now, from the hotel round the corner.' We were running up the road. 'I'll stay with the man, you run on. It's the White Swan Hotel.'

I could see him now, I could see the man lying inert in the road. He was half on his side, one arm outflung. The girl sprinted ahead. I kept on running. . .running and running. . .running towards the man. But I moved in a nightmare, my legs and feet dragged, the whole of me was weighted, for I knew who it was, I knew who I'd find. I had caught a glimpse of his raincoat—a light raincoat. . .

The man in the road was Nick.

CHAPTER FOUR

I LET out my breath on a hiss of relief as my fingers felt a pulse in his neck. He was still unconscious, but stirred as I spoke his name. 'Nick, it's all right.' I bent low to him. 'Nick, it's all right, it's Kate. You've had an accident, been struck by a car, but you're going to be all right. The ambulance will be here in a minute, try not to move.'

'What. . .? I don't. . .' He tried to sit up, then fell back again with a groan. 'Kate, my arm, my side. . . I can't. . .'

'It's all right, Nick, keep still, you must keep still. It's important not to move.'

He rolled a little, nearly on to his face. I was all but lying beside him. The rain fell on us, cars were stopping, people were crowding round. The girl driver was back, kneeling beside me, then I heard the ambulance, saw it backing into position, saw a police car and motorcycle, and more people, lights everywhere.

I had a feeling of complete unreality, as though I were dreaming it all. The road glistened like a seal's back; it was the same colour too; the ambulance men were getting their stretcher out. It was then that my training took over and I was able to be detached. 'I'm a doctor,' I told them. 'The casualty's name is Nicholas Carrington. He has a right-sided injury, probably ribs; he was unconscious only briefly. His airway is clear and he's lucid, but there's pain when he breathes. I know him, I'm his fiancé, so I'll follow the ambulance in and give full details at the receiving desk.'

'Thanks, Doctor.' The elder of the two men made signs to the other one. 'We're going to have to move you, sir, get you on the stretcher. Don't try to help yourself, leave it all to us.'

It was over in seconds—Nick on the stretcher, being put in the ambulance, the doors being closed, the ambulance making its banshee wailing again, all the way down Hobson's Lane to the Square, and Princes Parade, and the General Hospital. . .and still the rain came down.

The crowd was dispersing, but the police remained, talking to the girl, whose name was Jane Aveling; she was very young, very frightened and wet, her pale face peering out between dark curtains of hair. She made her way over to me. 'They've told me to meet them at the hospital.' She jerked her head towards the two policemen. 'Perhaps I'll see you there.'

'Well, that's where I'm bound for,' I said brusquely, forcing back a strong desire to tell her off for *daring* to run Nick down. She must have been speeding, then skidded and hit him. The road surface was lethal. I felt very sick, and because I did, and because, by the look of her, she did too, I said nothing except, 'See you in Casualty,' then drove off in the wake of the ambulance.

Being Saturday night, Casualty was even more busy than usual. There were people queuing at each of the three big reception desks. The chairs were all taken in the waiting area, a child was screaming its head off, while the reception clerks—imperturbable amid all the fracas—tapped away at their computer keyboards, taking down vital details.

I knew Nick would have been taken straight through

to the RTA Section. Pulling rank a little, I asked to see Sister and gave his details to her. Then I rang Alma from one of the pay-phones, which wasn't a task I relished. When I told her as carefully as I could what had happened, there was no sound at all from her end for a good ten seconds, then, 'Kate, for God's sake, how bad is he?' she gasped.

'Truly, Alma,' I made my voice calm, 'he doesn't seem too badly hurt. The doctors are with him, he'll be X-rayed, then we'll know the worst.'

'Well, I'm coming, I'm coming now! I'll use Nick's car. I'll be with you in twenty minutes!'

'Just be careful,' I said, but could have saved my breath for she'd slammed down the telephone.

Next I rang Aunt Laura, for she had to know where I was. She sounded nearly as upset as Alma. 'Oh, Kate, how awful! Is he badly injured?'

'A matter of fractured ribs, I would guess.' I was trying to sound detached and failing completely, for Aunt Laura's voice held overtones of sympathy, which nearly broke me up. 'I'll ring again when I've any news, and tell you what's happening,' I choked. Putting the phone back on its hook, I crossed to the waiting area. Jane Aveling was there, more chairs were brought, and we were able to sit down. Shortly afterwards Alma joined us, and a young, sandy-haired doctor with a freckled face came out to see her—she being Nick's next-of-kin.

'Your son is in X-Ray now, Mrs Carrington; we'll know more when we see his films. From my examination, however, I would think he has two, maybe three, fractured ribs. He has bruising down his right side, including his face. He has also fractured his clavicle—his collarbone, in other words.'

'I know what a clavicle is,' Alma snapped, and I knew how she felt, for doctors were rather apt to treat lay people like fools. 'How on earth did you come to run him down?' she asked Jane Aveling. 'I expect you were driving hell-for-leather, the way you young people do.'

'I was well within the speed limit, Mrs Carrington,' the girl defended herself. 'Your son stepped straight out from the kerb. I had no chance at all of avoiding him, especially on that wet road.'

Alma was silent, and so was I. Jane Aveling went to talk to the police officer who had just come in and was looking round for her. She had returned by the time we got the news that X-Ray had confirmed the young doctor's diagnosis; he came out to tell us so. Nick was sent up to the orthopaedic unit on the first floor. Alma and I were allowed to see him. He looked awful, he really did. The right side of his face was already beginning to swell. When he was struck by the car, he must have been flung up, then pitched face down— hence the broken clavicle, the kind of break steeple-chase jockeys so often sustain. He was under sedation and already half asleep, and as the hovering night staff plainly wanted us out we took our leave and tiptoed from the ward. 'He didn't look very comfortable, the way they've got him lying,' Alma said fretfully, rubbing her eyes, as we went down the flight of stairs.

'It's the best position for a collarbone fracture,' I told her, taking her arm. 'That pillow between his shoulders is to hold the bone-ends in place till tomorrow, when he'll be bandaged in a special kind of brace. I don't suppose they wanted to disturb him too much tonight.'

'What about his ribs?'

Alma looked tired, I tightened my grip on her arm.

'They'll heal naturally without any bandaging.' I saw her into her car. 'Truly, Alma, he'll be all right.' I leaned in to her. 'I expect he'll be kept in for about a week, and then you'll have him home. His injuries are painful, but they aren't serious.' My voice wobbled a bit. The shock of it all was taking its toll, beginning to get to me. It was a relief when Alma drove off, and I could lean against a wall till my legs stopped feeling as though there was nothing below my knees.

Aunt Laura was waiting up for me when I got back to the Larches. 'There've not been any other calls, and I hope there won't be,' she said. 'You look terrible, Kate. Go and get into bed and I'll bring you a hot drink.'

It was half-past midnight, I noticed, yet I didn't feel I could rest. In the end we drank hot chocolate together, sitting in the kitchen. Aunt Laura insisted that the accident must have been the girl's fault. 'Nick doesn't drink, so it couldn't have been that, and he's not the kind of man to go flying across roads without looking.' I agreed with her on both counts. . .well, more or less. . .but I didn't blame the girl, having heard her story, which I felt to be the truth.

'I think,' I said, 'that Nick left the hotel, annoyed because I was so long. He's not the most patient of men, you know, and I expect he got fed up waiting, decided to cross over to Bridge Street to the taxi rank, and in the heat of the moment didn't do his kerb drill, and was ploughed into by Jane's car.'

'Kate. . .oh, dear, surely not!' Aunt Laura was shocked, probably because I was blaming Nick. 'Kate, darling, you're overwrought!'

'So, when it comes down to it,' I ploughed on, determined to unburden myself, 'the accident was my

fault, entirely my fault. We should have stayed in
tonight, then Nick wouldn't have been stranded, and
none of this would have happened.'

'You can go iffing and butting like that forever,' said
my aunt, which was very true, but I still kept on doing
it, fitfully, all through the night.

I rang up at breakfast-time to ask how Nick was, and
was told 'comfortable', which, unless a patient has
actually died, or is dying, is all most hospitals give. I
enquired about Jenny Staves, in Surgical, and was told
the same thing there. Oh, well, no matter, I thought, I
intended to visit them both, this afternoon, if possible.
I wondered what to take Nick.

Aunt Laura had asked Alma to lunch, and as she
wasn't too keen on driving Nick's car again I went to
Park Road to fetch her. I thought she looked strained,
and preoccupied, but she ate a reasonable lunch, and
was made much of by Aunt Laura, who was everyone's
comforter. She was looking forward to Uncle John
coming back this evening. 'This golfing weekend will
have done him a world of good,' she told Alma, who,
not surprisingly, wasn't very interested.

She and I set off for the hospital soon after two
o'clock. Once there I suggested that she visit Nick,
while I went to Surgical Block. I wanted to see how the
Staves child was faring, and I felt quite sure that Alma
would want to see Nick, for a little while, without my
being there.

Jenny had undergone surgery soon after her admittance the evening before, but by then, as I'd feared,
peritonitis had generalised. She was on drips and
drains, and a naso-gastric tube was taped to her temple.
She was propped high in a sitting position; her round
child's face had thinned overnight, her skin looked old,

and she was holding her mother's hand. I was, however, told by the ward sister, whom I was lucky to find in her office, that the surgeons were pleased with her progress so far. . .'But she had a terrible abdomen. . .it was just as well that you had her admitted at the double, Dr Chalmers. . .another hour and the child might have died.'

'Yes,' I said, 'yes, she might.' And I could have kissed her for those kind words. At least some good had come out of last night's awful events.

Mr and Mrs Staves thanked me for what I had done. 'And for coming up here to see her, Doctor; we appreciate it, you know. Will you let Dr Masefield know what's happened?' Mr Staves asked. I promised I would, and made a note to go to Theodore Road and write a report later that afternoon.

The wind tore at my coat and scarf as I crossed the hospital yard to the northerly entrance marked 'Orthopaedic Block'. The ward Nick was in was a Nightingale type, with two long rows of beds, and it looked very full and untidy, as ortho wards frequently do. There were plastered legs suspended in frames, plastered legs lying flat, there were arms strung up, and arms strapped to chests, there were slings and bandages. Crutches and walking-aids leaned against lockers; wheelchairs blocked the aisles. There were visitors at most of the beds, some of them having to move and draw their chairs in as ambulant patients wanted to pass by.

Nick was sitting out of bed—topless, apart from a dressing-gown, which had been draped about him—and I saw that his shoulders had been braced back into a special bandage, a figure-of-eight type, with pads under his armpits to corectly align his bone. His face on the right side was puffed and purple, his right eye all but closed. He looked as though he had been in a fight. Even his hair was untidy, and somehow, for him, this was the biggest difference of all, and I wanted to burst into tears. Out of the two of us, Alma was the calmer. 'I'll go off now.' She kissed Nick. 'You and Kate will want to talk.'

'I've been thinking about you all night, Nick,' I told him as we clasped hands. 'How are you feeling? Are you very uncomfortable?'

'Yes, these bandages are so tight that they chafe.' He was sitting bolt upright.

'They have to be tight, or they wouldn't do their job,' I told him gently, 'and you'll have to wear that collar and cuff sling for a few weeks, I'm afraid. Anyway——' I dived into my bag '—I've brought you some books, they'll help pass the time, and Aunt Laura sent her love.' I put the books on his locker, then chanced my arm and asked, 'Nick, how did it happen—the accident, I mean? I'm sure everyone's been asking you that, but. . .how did it happen?' I repeated the question, meeting his gaze head on.

'I was jay-walking, mulling over all we'd talked about,' he said pointedly, putting the ball directly into my court.

'But why on earth did you leave the hotel? I wasn't *that* long,' I said defensively, then remembered his condition, and made myself calm down.

'It seemed long. I felt a bit silly being walked out on in public. Oh, and by the way,' he said, before I could speak, 'that girl, the driver, the one who hit me, rang up to ask how I was.'

'Yes, she was very upset and frightened, but soon got

herself together. She feels responsible.' As I did, and *do*, I added to myself.

'She couldn't have avoided hitting me,' Nick went on. 'If she'd been speeding, I'd have been dead by now. As it is, I'll probably be in here for another five days, then off work for a month. It's going to hold us up house-hunting; I can't deal with agents or view properties looking as I do.'

'The house-hunting can wait, there's no hurry,' I said, and as I spoke the words I knew I was glad and relieved to have a breathing space. Now this shocked me, even alarmed me, for what did it signify—surely not that I was having second thoughts about getting married? It couldn't be that, not possibly, yet somehow or other Nick and I seemed different now that we'd come back to Seftonbridge. We were a far cry from the carefree, happy-go-lucky couple who had talked, and laughed, and made plans. . .and love, last autumn in Gloucestershire. 'The main thing,' I managed to say, 'is to get you well again.'

'He looks awful, doesn't he?' Alma said brokenly, as I drove her back to Park Road.

'Yes,' I said shortly, for I couldn't deny it.

'And don't say it could have been worse, or I shall scream at you!' she burst out.

'I know how you feel.' I put on speed and began to pass a bus.

'If only he'd waited for you, Kate, not gone charging off.'

'Yes, if only.'

'Had you quarrelled again, during your meal, I mean?'

I was disconcerted when she said this—especially the word, 'again', for it was obvious that Nick must have mentioned our disagreement in town. Rightly or wrongly, I felt he should *not* have. It was between him and me.

'We had one or two things to sort out,' I said briefly. 'There was no quarrel, as such.' It was four-thirty, and getting dusk, so I switched on my lights. A party of hikers crossed the road, making for the station.

'You and Nick were made for one another,' Alma went on, 'so don't let a little thing like your work come between you, Kate. If you didn't work at all, after marriage, you wouldn't want for anything. Nick has a good position, and that's not likely to change.'

'My work's not a little thing to me, Alma, it's a hard-won career,' I said with restraint, 'but it won't come between us; we've effected a compromise.' I could have said more, but managed to bite down hard on my tongue. She couldn't help clucking, most mothers did it, and one day, maybe, I'd be the same when Nick and I had a child.

'It's not that I mean to interfere,' she said in a small, sad voice, 'but I do so want to see Nick settled; he deserves a good family life. His marriage to Lorraine wrecked his peace and destroyed his confidence. That sort of thing hangs about for a long time afterwards. I was so delighted, so relieved, when he got engaged to you.'

'Alma, it will be all right,' I said, then wondered what I was promising. For all I knew, Nick might have been the cause of his broken marriage. He might have been intolerant of Lorraine's job, even jealous of her success. Some men were like that. I didn't think Nick was. . .in fact, I was *sure* he wasn't. 'Don't worry,' I told her again, 'everything will work out.'

Ten minutes later I was drawing up outside her

house, next door to my old home, where Tom, Nick and I had first met, and formed a trio, and rioted about in the long old-fashioned garden. I glanced over at it now. It was nearly dark; shadows flitted, the wind soughed through the trees, calling, perhaps, for those boisterous children who were now grown-up, who were children no longer, and never would be again.

I saw Alma in, switched on her lights, and kissed her goodbye. I felt a surge of affection for her, and as I drove back to the Larches the annoyance I'd felt at her interference vanished without trace.

Aunt Laura had got the whole house lit up in welcome for Uncle, who was due at any minute, and I knew that the sitting-room curtains wouldn't be closed until he was safely inside. 'How did you find Nick?' She straightened up from the oven with a tray of scones in her hands.

'Reasonably well, on the whole, but every movement causes him pain. Alma's very upset, of course.'

'Well, she would be, wouldn't she?' my aunt said, moving the scones to a rack. 'How long will he be in hospital?'

'I would think about a week.' I sat down, then got up again, I didn't feel able to settle. 'If you don't mind,' I said, 'I'll go along to James's surgery and write up Jenny Staves's notes. I shan't be long—back for supper, anyway.' I turned towards the door.

'Do you have to go now?' Aunt Laura tutted, as she dropped a scone on the floor. It broke, and steamed and smelled of dates—a weakness of Uncle John's.

'Yes, I have to go now, because James will be back, or he will be very soon, and he'll need to have the details. I want to write them up while they're still fresh.'

'Talk about a new broom.' Aunt Laura sounded

cross. 'It seems to me that sweeping clean is one of the Chalmers traits.' As she said this she got on with sweeping up the bashed scone, and I made my way quietly out of the house while the going was good.

CHAPTER FIVE

MRS SHINWAY opened the door to me when I got to
Theodore Road. She was holding fast to Rollo's collar,
and asked me in at once. 'Can I get you a cup of tea,
Doctor?' She showed me into the surgery, switching on
the lights, and drawing the curtains. I crossed to the
cabinets.

'No, it's all right, thank you, Mrs Shinway.' I found
Jenny's notes, and sat down at the desk with them. 'I
shan't be very long.'

She bustled off, taking Rollo with her, and I was left
alone in the pleasant bay-windowed room, with the
velvet curtains drawn. I could imagine James seeing
patients here, sitting where I was now, in the same
chair, looking attentive and kind. The room seemed to
hold his presence, his white coat hung on the door, his
stethoscope, neatly looped together, lay on a glass-
topped trolley. Just in front of the desk—I marked the
spot—was where I had dropped the keys and bumped
heads with James, and forgotten the pain as I'd thrilled
to his nearness and touch.

Oh, stop dreaming, I told myself, pulling out Jenny
Staves's notes from the thick NHS envelope, and starting to fill in details of her illness, to bring James up-to-
date. I had just finished, and was about to leave an
alerting note for James, when I heard the front door
being opened, heard his voice and the child's. My heart
leapt; I'd not thought he would be home as early as
this. I was locking the cabinet when he came in. Eloise

was still in the hall with her arms round the dog; I could see her there, kneeling on the floor. Mrs Shinway took charge of her, stopping her coming through with James. 'Your father's busy; you come with me. It's good to see you, Doctor.' She beamed at him, then quietly closed the door.

'To quote Mrs Shinway, good to see *you*, Dr Kate!' He came further into the room, and stood directly under the light. 'Has there been some dire happening, or were you just returning the keys?' He was smiling, but I got the feeling he was making an effort to do so. He looked weary, older too, travel-worn and creased. It was a fair journey from Lewes to Seftonbridge, and the traffic on a Sunday was probably heavy and there'd be the Dartford tunnel to get through too. I wished— and this was ridiculous—that I could get his tea for him, and watch him drink it, and make a fuss of him. I wondered where the fair-haired Helen was, in her harebell-blue suit. Most likely James had dropped her off at her flat in Bateman Street. I knew she lived over the dental surgery. Aunt Laura had told me that.

'As a matter of fact there have been one or two unexpected happenings,' I told James as we faced one another over by the cabinets.

'Sit down and tell me about them. You look as played-out as I feel.' He said this with no alarm in his voice, but his glance at me was keen.

I sat down in the patients' chair, and he moved to the desk, sliding into his swivel chair, resting his hands on its arms. Briefly I told him about Jenny Staves. I got out the notes again, and passed them to him; he read them carefully. 'Oh, dear, poor child,' he said. 'What a good thing the father had the sense to ring for help, and what a good thing you acted promptly. She could have died if there'd been any further delay. Thank you for what you did.'

'All in the line of duty,' I said, then, afraid that he might think me flippant, I told him I'd seen Jenny that afternoon. 'Sister said that the surgeons are very pleased with her progress so far.'

'Who operated?'

'Mr Allan Bardwell.'

James rounded his mouth. 'Lucky to get *him* on a Saturday night.'

'Yes, so I was told.'

Neither of us said anything for a few seconds. James's fingers were rustling the notes, then, glancing up from them, he looked straight at me. 'Again, many thanks,' he said. 'I'm very grateful, and I'm sure the Staveses were, and to go to the hospital as well, to see the child, was a caring thing to do.'

'I was there anyway,' I informed him bluntly. 'I was visiting Nick—he had an accident on Saturday night.' I explained what had happened, in outline at first, then in greater detail. I was somehow impelled to talk, to let it all out to this listening stranger, for that was what James was, a stranger to me. I had known him a matter of days only, yet I couldn't hold back when it came to confiding in him.

'Oh, Kate,' he said at the end of it all, 'I'm so sorry! What more can I say?'

'Not a lot.' I kept tears at bay by concentrating hard on the calendar just behind James's head, and forcing myself not to blink. 'Seeing Nick lying in the road was the worst, seeing him lying so still. I could have *killed* that girl who ran him down; I was full of a terrible rage. Afterwards, though, I felt differently. She wasn't at fault. And Nick has admitted he was wool-gathering.

Well, you know how it is when you've a lot of things to think about—worries to resolve.'

'I do, yes, only too well——' James got up from his chair and sat nearer to me on the corner of the desk '—although Nick is very lucky to have you to help him sort out his problems.'

I smiled, but said nothing, for I *was* the problem, or my aims and objects were, and I could resolve that problem at a single stroke by giving in to Nick.

'Will his accident put your marriage plans back?' James was still sitting close. If I moved my hand only a matter of inches, it would rest against his thigh. I wanted it to do so. It was crazy, I knew; it was crazy and unforgivable, but I wanted to touch him so much that I had to restrain myself not to do so, and by the same token—even more so, perhaps—I wanted him to touch me.

'Yes, it will put our plans back.' I moistened dry lips to form the words. 'As Nick says, he can't view houses trussed up in bandages. He's very particular, he'll want to inspect everything inch by inch. He'll want to go up in the loft and take the lids off the tanks, and stick a knife in the rafters and floorboards; he's a very thorough type. We hoped to marry in June or July, but I doubt if we'll make that now.'

'So what will you do when you finish your locum?'

'Get another, I suppose, to fill up the gap. I can't just sit and wait. What I'd like is to go for a partnership, but I have to bear in mind what Nick wants, which is only fair, of course.'

'What *does* he want?' James's voice came softly.

'It's more what he doesn't want. He doesn't want a working wife. He says he doesn't mind, but he does, really—deep down he does, and there is a reason for it. He was married before to someone who put her work before him. . .' I stumbled on, feeling disloyal; forgive me, Nick, I breathed. But I had to tell someone, confide in someone, and James was a fellow doctor, he would know how I felt; he might even proffer advice. 'Of course,' I continued, 'he wouldn't stop me practising, he's not the dominant kind, but if I insisted on carrying on I'm pretty sure that everything that went wrong between us would be blamed on my having a job.'

'I think you're right,' James remarked, out of the silence that followed.

'I know I am.' I bit my lip. He wasn't helping much. And perhaps he sensed my disappointment, perhaps it showed in my face, for he half smiled and touched my shoulder:

'What is it you want from me, Kate—an opinion, or advice? You can have them both, for what they're worth.' He got up from the desk and went to stand by the line of cabinets, one arm along their tops. 'My opinion is that it would be a great shame to give up your career. We need good doctors, the whole world needs them, we can't easily spare *one*. As for my advice, ask yourself if you care for Nick deeply enough to give up everything for him. Women have done it before, you know—and so have men. You know that age-old saying—the world well lost for love. Even thrones have been given up for it. It's a very powerful force.'

'Yes, I know.' I looked at the carpet. There had been something in his eyes, and in his voice, when he'd said the word 'love' that robbed me of my breath. He was too attractive—disturbingly so. He could make me feel a totally different person. And that's not what I want at

all, I thought, getting to my feet, and turning away to
pull on my gloves, just as Mrs Shinway came in.

'Tea's ready, Doctor, set out in the sitting-room, and
Eloise should be having hers now, she's very tired.' Her
soft voice held reproach.

'Point taken, I'm coming.' James walked round to
face me. 'Stay and have some with us, Kate. We'd like
that, wouldn't we, darling?' he said to Eloise, who had
come in followed by the dog.

In no way did the child enthuse. She treated me, at
first, to a long stare, narrowing her eyes, as though to
get me in focus. 'Yes,' she said eventually, but the
paucity of her reply was made up for by her beguiling
smile, which split her small face in two.

'It's tea and a half on Sundays,' said her father. 'It's
the one day of the week when I'm reasonably sure to
be in for it, and we always have it together, don't we,
Lou?' He passed a hand over her head.

I could have made an excuse, I suppose, but I didn't,
I decided to stay. And it turned out to be the kind of
tea we used to have at home—Tom and I, when we
were small—and it really took me back. It was set out
on a low round table in a room across the hall. There
was a 'real' coal fire, and leathery chairs, while a bowl
of freesias combined their flowery perfume with the
down-to-earth one of tea. There were sandwiches and
scones, a big fruit cake, and a wobbly green jelly in the
shape of a rabbit, made especially for Eloise.

Mrs Shinway poured out, then left us to it. I felt
rather awkward at first. I wasn't used to children and
didn't feel I was good with them. James was a perfect
host, though, passing everything in sight, serving Eloise
with her jelly, and asking me about the practice I'd
worked in at Cheltenham; he really seemed interested.

'I don't know Gloucestershire myself.' He loaded a scone with jam. 'I came here from London five years ago, when Eloise was two. My wife worked, freelance—she was able to do it from home. She was an artist, illustrated children's books and magazines.'

'Oh, *did* she?' I was on to that at once, for I had artistic leanings myself. I wanted to know more about it, *and* her. What had James's wife been like?

'We've still got some of Mummy's drawings and paintings, haven't we, Lou?' He smiled across at the child, who nodded with her mouth full.

Chewing hard, and swallowing rapidly, she asked if she could get down. James told her she could, and she scudded off, as though with some purpose in mind.

'Does she remember her mother?' I asked, then wondered if, perhaps, I ought to leave the subject alone. Yet he had brought it up.

'Oh, yes, she does,' he replied, readily enough. 'She was four when Colette was killed, so was out of the baby stage. We often talk about her; I feel it's right to do so——' He broke off as Eloise came back with a folder in her hand. She opened it, and handed me the painting that lay inside.

'That's Mummy,' she told me importantly, coming to stand at my side. 'It's a safe portrait, she did it in front of the glass.'

'A *self*-portrait,' James said, laughing, but I hardly heard his words. I was too busy looking at the 'safe portrait' of a girl with chestnut hair curling about her face like petals, a girl with a full sweet mouth, and a dimple in her chin, a girl with smiling eyes.

'It's lovely,' I said, 'really lovely, Eloise. You had a very pretty mummy.'

'She used to smell nice too.' She took the portrait and put it back in the folder.

James laughed as he watched her go out with it. 'Painting your own portrait is a little like writing your autobiography, or at least, so I would think. The bits you don't like you can leave out, or alter.' He still looked amused.

'Isn't it a good likeness, then?'

'No, not really,' he said. 'It's recognisable, but only just. Colette did it for fun, one wet Sunday afternoon, and gave it to Lou, who took it to play-school, puffed up with pride, for three weeks afterwards. Colette was better at painting other people—at painting out of her head, painting her dreams, as she used to say——' Once again he broke off, as Eloise came back, empty-handed this time, rather to my relief.

It was then that I mentioned my own attempts at sketching and painting. 'But with me it's just a hobby,' I emphasised. 'Nick thinks it's rather a joke. I've no real talent, but it's therapeutic, takes my mind off blood and guts!'

James laughed, then sobered. His face was expressive, and could change in a flash from laughter to gravity. 'What kind of sketching?' he asked.

'Seascapes when I'm near the sea, riverscapes when I'm not. I love painting water, trying to capture the shades of reflected light.'

'Good! Doctors need a side-kick to keep them sane,' he remarked. 'Talent doesn't matter. The urge to create is a gift in itself. When the weather gets warmer you'll be able to set your easel up near Challoner's Bridge. I've often seen artists working down there—some of them students, trying to lift the pressures of exams.'

There was an audible sigh from Eloise. She was

either bored with adult conversation, or tired and ready for bed. Making an effort to draw her into the conversation, I asked her where she went to school.

'St Mary's in Silver Street,' she was quick to reply. She was a very bright little girl. 'Mr Shinway takes me in his car before he goes to the hospital. It's on his way, so it's no bother. Daddy fetches me home, or, if he can't, Mrs Shinway comes out on the bus.'

'I know St Mary's, but I always thought it was a boarding school,' I said. The fire did a downward shunt in the grate, and I took a quick peep at my watch. I ought to be going, it was nearly six-thirty, and Aunt Laura wouldn't be pleased if I was late back for the special supper she'd prepared.

'It takes day pupils as well,' supplied James, pushing back his chair. 'Sorry, Kate, if you'll excuse me, I'll go and fetch some more coal. I don't like disturbing the Shinways on a Sunday evening.' Seizing the scuttle, he made tracks for the door.

I felt that this was a good moment to make my exit too, but he was gone and closing the door before I could so much as frame the words. Eloise was bent on talking to me; she had lost her earlier shyness. 'When Daddy marries Helen she'll live here,' she told me, 'then I'll be a boarder, like lots of my friends. I don't think I shall mind.'

'I should imagine it could be fun,' I said brightly, and before James came back I tried to arrange my face in a way that would hide the feelings behind it. What I felt most was a sense of inevitability, for I had guessed he was destined for Helen. I also felt relief that he was out of reach, for surely, surely, knowing this, I would no longer feel his bewitching effect on me. As well as these two things, however, I felt surprise and dismay that he was even so much as *contemplating* allowing his daughter to board. Seven years old was too young for that, and he of all people must know it; what was he thinking about? I thought less of him, and was glad I did, for thinking less of him helped. When he came back into the room I gave him a long, hard stare, which was, however, lost on him, for he was looking straight at the fire. He went and knelt down by it, shovelling on the coal.

'I must be going,' I said, at the exact second that the telephone rang in the hall. I could hear Mrs Shinway answering it, then she tapped and came into the room.

'It's Mrs Chalmers, the doctor's wife.' She sounded like Happy Families. 'She asked to speak to you, Dr Kate. It's concerning one of Dr Masefield's patients.'

'In that case, as I'm back, I can deal with it.' James got up from the hearth. He left the door open as he went out, and I walked through into the hall. I heard him speaking to Aunt Laura, and thanking her, then he was putting down the phone. 'It's one of my elderly asthmatics in trouble; his wife can't cope. I'll have to go—sorry, Kate.'

'Don't mention it,' I said. I hoped I sounded a little frosty, but, once again, I don't think he noticed.

'Thanks again for your help; I'm grateful.' He was shrugging into his coat. 'Look after Dr Kate, Mrs Shinway, and goodnight, little poppet.' He kissed Eloise, opened the front door and was gone.

Eloise yawned and sat down on the stairs, picking at a thread on her kilt. 'Daddy's always rushing off,' she said, as I reached for my coat.

'Well, he has to look after ill people, doesn't he?' I felt for my keys.

'I s'pose so,' she nodded. 'Are you coming again?'

'If I'm needed,' I told her, shaking my head in response to Mrs Shinway's offer of a fresh brew of tea. 'It's kind of you, but I ought to get home.' I smiled down into her round, bespectacled face. 'My uncle is only just back from a weekend away, and we have things to talk about—like, for instance, tomorrow's surgeries. I'm quite sure you know how it is.'

'Oh, indeed I do,' she replied. 'I've worked in doctors' households all my life, even before I was married, but this is the first time I've had a little girl to look after as well.' She passed a hand over Eloise's hair, smoothing it back from her face. 'And I wouldn't be without her for all the tea in China!' She hugged the child, and I could have hugged her for doing so; she was a very kind woman. Most likely she had 'mothered' Eloise ever since her mother was killed.

A few minutes later, driving back to the Larches, I made a firm resolve to put James and his daughter, and his affairs and problems, right out of my thoughts. Whatever he did, or decided to do, was nothing to do with me. . .

All I had been was his stand-in for the weekend.

CHAPTER SIX

NICK was discharged home on the following Saturday, when he came under the care of the district nursing service, much to Alma's relief. 'I'd be afraid to touch him,' she said, 'I'd be hopeless as a nurse.'

She had been looking very unwell since Nick had his accident. Their GP was Charles Ridgeway, whom I had met at the Roseveares' party. I urged her to consult him, but she insisted that she was all right. 'It's just the shock,' she said, 'I'm still not over it. . . I mean, Nick might have been killed.'

He had been home nearly a week, and I was seeing him most days, when I got a telephone call from James. Thinking that he was going to ask me to stand in for him again, I was considerably taken aback when he invited me to Eloise's birthday party. 'It's on Saturday,' he said, 'so terribly short notice, but I promised Lou I'd ask you. She's very anxious for you to come.'

'Oh, well, that's flattering!' I said, giving a nervous laugh, while I searched around for an excuse not to go, for hadn't I resolved not to get any more involved with the Masefields than I needed? Anyway, what about Helen Clifford? Surely she was the one to go. . . probably *was* going, anyway, so, 'I'm sorry, but. . .' was right on the tip of my tongue, but before I could give it breath James broke in with,

'Naturally enough, I'd love you to come, but I know your fiancé is out of hospital now, and probably you'll be wanting to spend Saturday with him.'

So there was my excuse, but I didn't take it. Instead I heard myself saying, 'Well, I *am* due to have supper with him and his mother on Saturday night, but so long as I leave your house by eight that would be quite all right.'

'Kate, that's wonderful. . .if you're really sure.'

'Couldn't be more so,' I said, and laughed again, for he'd sounded pleased, and welcoming, and warm.

'Come about four,' he added, 'and don't worry about getting away. Seven-thirty marks the end of the programme. Lou knows that.'

I asked if I could help with the preparations, but was told that Mrs Shinway would be arranging all the food side, while he was in charge of games. 'I'll be MC,' he said, 'but, believe you me, I'm going to need your assistance. It'll be no mean task entertaining twenty ebullient kids. By the time the whole thing is over, we'll be halfway up the wall!'

So it was to be him and me—*just* him and me—I thought with satisfaction, and a stirring excitement, as I said we'd cope, before I put down the phone.

Armed with a suitable gift for Eloise—a colouring book and crayons—I drove to Theodore Road on Saturday, all ready for the fray. Most of the guests—boys and girls mixed—had arrived when I got there, and were in the sitting-room playing a pre-tea game of I-spy. I hardly recognised the sitting-room, for all the furniture had been shifted—chairs and sofas pushed back to the walls, extra chairs brought in, occasional tables and ornaments sensibly removed. There was a wide expanse of carpet in the middle—'Behold, the arena,' James said, while Eloise, strikingly pretty in emerald green, jumped up to say hello. I gave her her present, which she immediately unwrapped.

'Oh, thank you, I like this sort of thing,' she said in her grown-up way. Her smile told me she meant what she said, but I could also tell, as she backed away, that she was trying to avoid any sudden move from me. I knew how she felt, for I could well remember being seven years old, and having to submit to hugs and kisses that I often didn't want.

'She's losing her front teeth,' James remarked as she went back to join I-spy, 'so the tooth fairy has been paying up at twenty pence a time.'

'She's going to be stunning when she grows up.' I watched her taking her seat beside Rollo, keeping a protective hand on his head.

'She has my colouring and her mother's features.' James was taking me through to the dining-room for a sight of the birthday tea. I gasped when I saw it, for Mrs Shinway had certainly excelled herself. There were burger-sized rolls filled with ham and cheese, sausages on sticks, peanut butter sandwiches, dishes of crisps. There were chocolate biscuits, and a coffee log cake, jellies in three different colours, a trifle with cherries and nuts and cream, and an army of gingerbread men.

'While the *pièce de resistance*,' James whispered, 'is through in the kichen.' There we found Mr Shinway, dragging off his wellies, while on one of the work-tops rested a cake, dartboard-sized in diameter, white-iced, piped in pink, with seven candles on top. 'And here——' James dived into his pocket '—is a list of games I've got out. Even with a kids' party I like to be organised. . .*especially* with a kids' party,' he added, as the sound of a violent argument and a cry of, 'That's rude, I'll tell Mummy you said that!' came from the sitting-room. 'Let's get them through to tea *now*,' he said, and that was what we did.

There were place-names against each setting, which the children loved. Eloise was at the head of the table, her father at the foot. I was halfway down on one side, next to a little girl who asked me if I was Lou's mummy, but before I could answer her a sharp little boy with a fierce black fringe told her not to be daft. 'Lou hasn't got a mum, she's dead, because my mum said!'

I didn't look at James, but I felt for him, for, even after so many years, a remark like that, coming out so pat, must have had an effect. But children are tough, and it had none on them, there was no difficult silence. All Eloise said was, 'Yes, that's right,' whereafter the talk centred on how many presents she'd had, and how much they had cost. One child, who clearly thought she had the edge on everyone, said she'd had a parrot for her birthday and was 'learning' him to talk.

'*Teaching* him,' Eloise corrected, while the black-fringed little boy, who had eaten at least four sausages and was rasping into crisps, said he'd had a computer for Christmas, which capping remark kept everyone silent till the cake was brought in, and 'Happy Birthday' was sung.

After the cake it was back to the sitting-room, where James and I arranged two rows of chairs back-to-back in the centre of the floor. The game, Musical Chairs, was announced by James in his MC voice. Acting under orders, I switched on the record-player, when, to the tune of 'Tulips from Amsterdam', the game got under way.

Blind Man's Buff followed, then Hunt the Slipper, then came a vociferous rendering of the Hokey Cokey—the calls being shouted out by James. He amazed me, he really did; he was plainly enjoying himself, and so was I.

Pin the Tail on the Donkey was a success too, but dancing the Conga was better—a snake of us, James and I included, conga-ing up and down the hall, into the dining-room, and up the stairs. A break was called, for cooling refreshments—squash and ice-cream, and more biscuits, paper plates catching *some* of the crumbs. I saw James loosening his tie once; he'd already flung off his jacket. Squashed between two little girls, another on my knee, I could only look round at him and smile, and make a 'phew' with my mouth. When he winked at me, I went three shades warmer in a rather different way, and I swear that my heart beat harder under the blue silk of my dress. He had so many sides to him, every one of them likeable, or did I mean lovable? He loved children, that was obvious; he could level with them, be as they were for a time. He didn't mind acting the fool, either, and the children shrieked with laughter when, later, during Pass the Parcel, he pretended the parcel was hot and batted it about from hand to hand, as though doing a juggling act.

But it was over at last, Mums and Dads arrived, and the children were going off, each with a goody-bag and a balloon, each with a small toy. There was a crowd in the hall, and a howling draught, then a dash out to the cars, and in the silence after they'd driven away I felt James's hand on my arm. 'I know you want to get off,' he said, 'but get your breath back first.'

'I think I must!' We went into the sitting-room and sat down on the couch. Eloise was on the hearthrug, sorting through her gifts, Rollo beside her, a screwed-up ball of paper between his paws. 'It was a good party.' I stared at James's sleeve, which had a smudge of black on its cuff.

'It was the *best ever*!' Eloise jumped up and gave her

father a kiss, as she saw Mrs Shinway in the doorway, waiting to take her to bed.

'Aren't you going to thank Kate for helping to make it the best party ever?' James asked, disentangling his daughter's arms from his neck.

'Yes, thank you very much,' she said, standing in front of my knees, rubbing the toe of her silver pump against the back of her leg.

'I enjoyed it too. I thought it was smashing.' I smiled and leaned towards her. I was expecting nothing, but what I got was a quick shy kiss, followed by a stranglehold hug, which brought a great loop of my hair cascading down from its loose knot. And then she was off, flying towards Mrs Shinway, who hustled her upstairs, talking about a quick wash, and then into bed with you.

'My boisterous daughter!' I felt James's eyes on me, as I hastily thrust my disarranged hair under what remained of my knot. It wouldn't stay there, of course, but it might just hold till I got into the car. Having it partly hanging down made me feel vulnerable.

'She's a very sweet girl.' I got to my feet. Sitting close to James wasn't a good idea at all; besides, it was time I was off.

'So are you, sweet Kate.' He was standing too, smiling straight into my eyes, arms hanging lax at his sides. He didn't touch me, didn't draw me close, but it seemed to me, as we gazed, that kisses sparked and lit between us. . .were there for the taking. . .not the thank-you kind, nor the childish kind, but the heart-stopping, blissful kind that could make magic, or wreak havoc, or do both at the same time.

'I ought to be going; Nick will be waiting.' I said that deliberately, because I had to keep my feelings in check, even though I was sure he had seen what they were, for my face is the kind that doesn't block things off.

'Of course—let's get your coat, shall we?' I fancied he sounded relieved. After all, he had Helen to think about, so how fortunate it was that we'd not succumbed to our baser instincts and gone into a clinch.

Once in the hall he reached for my coat, and helped me into it. My hair tumbled down again as he did so, but this time I didn't care. I'd be gone in a minute, and so I was, practically fleeing from him, calling out 'Super party!' like an idiot, getting into the car and driving off with a pip on the horn, just to show how blasé I was.

He's attractive, but then so is Nick, and it's Nick I love. The words drummed out like a refrain in my head as I drove swiftly towards Park Road.

After another fortnight Nick was free of bandages and could move about without pain, merely wearing his sling. He was anxious to start house-hunting, and during the week before he was due to start work again we found a property we liked. It was just off the Cletford Road, and had a distant view of the river. It was three-bedroomed, and detached, and there was room to extend, if we wanted to do so, in the future. The vendor—a Mrs Carlton, a widow—was anxious to sell, as she had already bought a flat at Frinton-on-Sea, and was on a bridging loan. 'I hope you won't let me down,' she said. She was a fierce-eyed woman, with a jaw like a man's, and cropped grey hair. This was said on our third visit there, when Nick had made an offer which had been accepted; he stared coolly back at her.

'There's no question of that, Mrs Carlton. Providing the survey is satisfactory and our solicitors work at speed, I could be ready to complete in a month or six weeks. There should be no snags at all.'

I had the strangest feeling when I heard him say that—an uneasy, panicky feeling—the sort of feeling you have when you're at the point of no return. I wanted to be married and I knew Nick did, we were conventional and family-minded, but ought we to be marrying *one another*? Had we allowed outside people—like Alma, for instance, and my brother, Tom—to point us towards marriage? Had we enough in common to weld us together 'till death us do part'? You haven't, have you, and you'll come to grief, a nasty little voice kept telling me at unguarded moments, especially in the night.

'You ought to be fixing a date, Doctor,' Doris Leigh, our receptionist, told me one morning when we were busy opening the mail. Aunt Laura had told her about the house Nick and I were buying. It wasn't all that far from where Doris lived, so she was very interested. 'Yes, you ought to fix a date, because of the reception,' she went on. 'Everywhere gets so booked up, especially between June and September, and then there's the church.'

'We're having a register office wedding. Nick's been divorced,' I told her shortly, 'and the reception will be back here at the Larches.'

'Oh, I see, I didn't realise that.' Doris's eyes loomed large behind her glasses; she was clearly very surprised. She was married herself, and had two teenage sons; her husband was a builder. Aunt Laura said his charges were moderate, and she had already got him earmarked for work on our house. Things were moving along very fast.

Doris sorted letters from lab reports, and handed the

two piles to me. 'You've got nineteen patients this morning——' she moved towards the door '—twenty with Mrs Barnes from Linton Grove. I squeezed her in last; I felt I should. She's preggers, she says—she did the test at home.'

'Oh, good.' I reached for my surgery coat.

'I doubt if she sees it that way. It's her fifth child in seven years.' Doris went through to the waiting-room, where she had her desk. I heard her pick up the phone.

The first patient, Dominic Harrison, came in in his carry-cot, carried by his mother who looked about seventeen. He was to have his first whooping cough jab; he lay blissfully asleep. 'Shall I get him out, Doctor?' his mother looked anxious.

'Yes, if you would,' I said. 'He won't feel much, but to wake him up with a prick wouldn't be very kind. Hold him on your lap and bare his thigh—I don't mind which one.'

I drew up the vaccine and injected him swiftly. He let out a yell, of course; most babies did, more in fury than pain. 'All done now,' I said. 'Rub it for him, then dress him again; he'll soon forget all about it.'

'He won't be ill, will he?'

'No, he'll be fine,' I assured the young mother. She had long, straight, mouse-coloured hair, which drooped over her baby as she pulled up his cream woollen trousers and put him back in his cot. 'The next injection is due when Dominic is six months old,' I said, 'then he'll need another at a year old, but they'll have explained that to you in Clinic.'

'Yes, they did, Doctor, thanks.' The child had stopped crying, and the girl looked relieved. I opened the door for her, filled in the baby's details on a card, and rang for the next patient, an arthritic eighty-year-old. His name was Harry Lowfield, he walked with a stick and clearly resented Doris helping him into the room.

'I can manage, girl!' I heard him snap, but that was nothing to the way he reacted when he set eyes on me. At first he said nothing at all, just stared at me with his mouth open, fronds of dry white hair falling about his ears and collar. 'What does this mean. . .who are you?' he shouted, raising his stick.

'I'm the doctor taking surgery.'

'But you're a woman!'

'Yes, that's true. Please sit down, Mr Lowfield. What can I do for you?'

He remained standing. 'I want Dr Chalmers.'

'I *am* Dr Chalmers—Dr Kate Chalmers.' I tried the effect of a smile.

'I want the one I always see. I want to see the man!' He glowered at me, and, bringing out his handkerchief, coughed with a cagging sound.

'Dr John Chalmers will be taking surgery this evening.'

'Then I'll come back then. I don't have no truck with women doctors. . .'tisn't decent, 'tisn't right! I don't know what the world's coming to! I'll come back tonight!'

There were titters from the waiting-room, and even I had to laugh, though not until the old man had thumped his way out of the house. Glancing through the window, I could see him limping down the drive; he even took a swipe at the hedge, as though to relieve his ire. 'What had he come about?' I asked Doris, feeling a little anxious.

'He's got a sore throat—"rough as a grater" was how

he described it. Now, why on earth couldn't he have let you see it? What's sexy about a throat?'

'Search me.' I shrugged and pulled the next patient's notes towards me. As my mother would have said— 'there's none sae queer as folk'. Even in these enlightened days, there was still some prejudice against women doctors. . .lots of men didn't like them, or felt embarrassed when faced with them.

The morning wore on, and it was after eleven before Mrs Barnes, the pregnant patient, came importantly into the consulting room. I asked her the usual questions, examined her on the couch, asked more questions, made calculations, then put down my pen. 'Your baby should be born during the third week in October,' I said. 'You'll know all the wrinkles, I'm quite sure, about booking in at the hospital, and attending the antenatal clinic.'

'I ought to, Doctor.' She smiled. 'I'm what you might call an old hand. I mean to stop at six, though, both Dick and I feel that's enough. Still, we wanted to have them while we were young. . .to be young with them.'

'I can see the advantages,' I said quietly, watching her hook up her skirt. Eileen Barnes was still under thirty, jowly and rosy-cheeked, with dark hair and slumbrous eyes, framed in fantastic lashes. Her eyes, I felt, had a lot to answer for.

It was a morning for babies, for when I went through to the living part of the house I found Aunt Laura with her arms wrapped round a tiny shawled infant. A tall, rather gaunt-looking girl in cords and a mohair sweater was on the settee drinking coffee, and I knew at once that she was Rose Spender—Dr Rose Spender—whose post I was filling till the end of May. She smiled as I approached.

When introduced we regarded one another with mutual interest. I looked at her baby too, of course, and said all the appropriate things. It was a girl baby, and she wasn't pretty—being long-faced and bald—but she had potential, she would blossom, I could see that at a glance. She would probably favour her mother, who had paintable cheekbones, a sweet expression, and lovely clean lines to her face.

'So, you're keeping my job warm for me, Kate,' she said, as I sat down.

'I'm doing my best.' We smiled at one another, and I liked the look in her eyes.

'I miss the patients, miss integrating with so many different types.' She took the baby from my aunt and held her upright against her shoulder, where she burped against her neck.

'How will you manage when you come back,' I asked, 'with the baby, I mean?'

'Oh, my mother lives with us, she'll take over; she can't wait, she says. The only thing is——' she rested her cheek against the infant's head '—you feel differently when you've had a baby; it changes you, you know. I want to come back here. . . I mean to say, I *am* a doctor. . .but I also want to do everything for Clarissa, bring her up myself. One feels very divided, somehow. Still——' she nuzzled her child '—how about you? You're getting married very soon, I hear.'

'Some time this summer,' I replied, 'and I shall carry on practising, but part-time only, which will simplify things at home.'

'What about children?'

'Oh, we want them eventually, and I expect, like you, I shall want to bring them up myself, but I'll cross that bridge when they start to arrive,' I added laughingly. Not that I felt like laughing, I felt a hundred years old—depressed and weighted, which was fairly unusual for me.

After Rose had gone, I went back into the surgery to collect my medical bag. I had two house-calls to make and then—being Thursday—the rest of the day was entirely my own. Doris usually left at half-past eleven, so I was rather surprised to see her still sitting at her desk when I peeped into the waiting-room. 'Are you catching up on something?' I asked her.

'No.' She got to her feet. She had taken off her glasses and her eyes looked smaller, the whole of her face drawn and worried, and it struck me then that there was something dreadfully wrong. 'Can you take one more patient this morning?' 'She gave me a strained half-smile. I knew she was on our patient-list, and I knew that she meant herself.

'Of course, Doris. . .come through, sit down. What seems to be the trouble?' She had put her notes out on the desk, and I drew them towards me.

'I've got a lump, Doctor. . .left breast. I noticed it three days ago. It doesn't seem very big, but it's there. I felt I'd rather see you than Dr John. . .you know how it is.'

'Yes, of course.' My heart sank: a breast lump—no wonder she was worried, poor woman. 'Let's get your blouse and bra off, shall we, and then I'll have a look.'

Her hands were shaking as she unfastened the buttons and I understood what she was feeling. She'd know only too well what her lump might be, for lay people, these days, are well genned-up on bodily functions and ailments of all kinds. Added to this, Doris was a medical secretary, and a keen one at that. She would pick up knowledge like a pecking sparrow, and, while knowledge is a very good thing, it can play havoc with one's peace of mind when illness strikes and known horrors draw up uncomfortably close.

Doris's lump was in the upper left quadrant of her breast. It was about the size of a plum-stone, and didn't appear to be attached to skin or muscle, and there was no axillary swelling.

'What do you think?' she asked anxiously as she got dressed again. 'There is a lump there. . .it's not just mastitis?'

'Yes, there is a lump, Doris,' I said carefully, 'but you've been very sensible and consulted me quickly, not pretended it isn't there. I'm going to refer you to Mr Ford-Hobbs at the Seftonbridge General. I'll write him a note, then you can ring through to his secretary for an early appointment. The sooner it's sorted out, the better, but, as I'm sure you know, only one in five women presenting with breast lumps are found to have carcinoma.'

'But whatever it is, it means surgery, doesn't it? I mean, they're bound to want it out.'

'I don't know,' I said cagily with my head down—I was filling up the referral form. 'I'm going up to the General now, so I can drop this in. In the meantime, try not to worry. I know that's a tall order, but worry achieves nothing, just makes matters worse, and you've done all the right things.'

'It could be benign.' She was looking more hopeful.

'Yes, of course it could. It could be a simple lipoma or cyst.'

'Then I wouldn't lose my breast, would I?'

'No, you'd have a lumpectomy.'

'That's just the sort of unglamorous thing I *would*

have,' said Doris, still looking worried, but managing a grin as well.

A few minutes later she went off on her bicycle, and I watched her go. After delivering the referral letter to the hospital, I made my two house-calls, and as it was Thursday, and my half-day, made plans for the afternoon. I would go down to the river, I decided; I would go down there and paint. It was warm for the middle of March—a perfect early spring day. I would make for Challoner's Bridge, and sit on the towpath and empty my mind of stress. There would be no one there, it being mid-week; I'd be left in peace. Even thinking about it during lunch made my spirits rise.

I set off at one-thirty, so as to get the best of the light. Aunt Laura tutted a bit as I stowed my materials away in the Renault. I'm sure she thought I was mad. 'Don't stay down there too long,' she called out. 'It's not as warm as it seems.'

CHAPTER SEVEN

CHALLONER'S BRIDGE was beautiful. It was over three hundred years old, built of grey stone with four arches, and just to look at it gave me a thrill. I parked the car and took out my sketching block, palette and paints. I never used an easel; I painted on my lap. I was very amateur, and the last thing I wanted was to attract attention. With a board on my knees, and the paper pinned to it, I could do a more private job.

I'd not painted a thing since Christmas, when I'd attempted a view of the Cotswolds; but I'd had to huddle, for it had been cold and windy, too cold for concentrating, and my clothes had balked me—I'd been muffled up to the ears.

There was no need for huddling today, for the sun was really warm. I stripped off, and sat on my folding stool in sweater and jeans. There was no one about. I could hear nothing but the distant hum of traffic, and the bird sounds, and the breeze in the reeds, and one or two ploppings that could have been made by fish or water voles. Even these sounds receded as I concentrated on capturing the way the water rippled under the bridge, the different patterns it made passing through each arch, and the way the light glimmered on the ancient stone. I had to get it right.

I had finished rough-sketching and was filling in the reeds and riverbank first, when a black and white lurcher dog came to sniff at my painting things. 'There's plenty of water in the river,' I told him, 'I want what's in that jar.' He looked at me with yellow eyes, then stretched himself beside me, resting his long skinny nose on his paws. I worked on, painting swiftly, before the light changed, before the excitement left me and the urge to create ran out. And presently, and unbelievably, the scene on my knees took life, became easily recognisable. It really *was* Challoner's Bridge. 'I'm improving,' I told the lurcher. 'I'm better than I used to be. Not only that, but I feel better in myself, which is far more to the point.'

I was washing out my brushes when I saw a man and a dog coming towards me. The dog was large and cream-coloured, the man tall and dark-haired, wearing a blue jersey over slim dark trousers. He was beyond the bridge, which meant that he was still some distance away, but I would have known him a mile off. It was James, with Rollo. I waited with fast-beating heart and a dry mouth, waving when he did, standing by my stool.

'Hello, Kate.' He halted in front of me, looking down at my brushes and palette. 'You've got your artist's hat on this afternoon.' His face creased into smiles.

'For a few hours, yes,' I said, 'it's my afternoon off.' I dried a brush and thrust it back in its box.

'Who's your lean friend?' He was looking at the lurcher.

'I've no idea,' I laughed, 'he just appeared from nowhere and joined me.' We sat down then, I on my stool, he on a piece of tree.

'How are you?' His gaze was direct, his eyes reflecting the blue of his jersey, which was the thick and chunky kind.

'Absolutely fine.' I fidgeted a little. Oh, why had he stopped? Why hadn't he just said hello and passed by, then I wouldn't feel disturbed like this.

'And Nick?' One of his eyebrows rose.

'Oh, fine,' I said, 'he's back at work now, there are no ill effects.'

'I'm glad, and I'm sure *you* are.'

'Yes, I am.' Our talk was choppy with no follow-ups. I swallowed and looked at the dogs, who had no communication problems; they sat side by side at James's feet.

'Jenny Staves made a good recovery.' And now he was talking shop, which was a good idea, and we discussed the various stages of Jenny's illness. After that he asked if he might be allowed to look at my painting. He asked with so much formality and diffidence that I burst out laughing.

'I shan't mind if you think it's terrible,' I said, 'you don't have to be polite—but it's still wet,' I added quickly. Not that I need have bothered, for he took it with care, and I wondered if perhaps, many times before, he had handled his wife's work like that. I waited for his verdict, not with bated breath exactly, but I nevertheless minded what he thought of my painting. I still had the trees to fill in.

'It's charming, Kate. You've brought it off.' He glanced at the bridge, then back again at the painting. 'Very well done indeed.'

'Thanks,' I said gruffly, as he handed it back. 'I was in the mood today—for painting, I mean. I needed to escape from the world of reality.'

'I think I did. . .in a way.' He paused, and I wondered why, wondered what he was going to say. But, whatever it was, he decided against it, merely adding, 'It's one of my favourite spots down here. We often come, don't we, Rollo?' He bent forward and fondled the Labrador's silky ears.

'Tom, Nick and I used to be brought on picnics here,' I said reminiscently. 'Nick's father was alive then. He was great with a punt—really skilful and graceful—sometimes we went right up to Byron's Pool.'

'I was forgetting you're a native of these parts.'

'Oh, yes, I was born here,' I said. 'I love it, and I'm glad I'll be making my home here all over again. It seems right that I should—like coming full circle; there's a pattern to it, somehow, and Nick and I have found a house at last.'

'Yes, your aunt told me that when I met her last week.' He was getting up to go, and so was Rollo, who was stretching, bending down low with his front half, his rear part wagging his tail. 'The house you're buying belongs to one of my patients, a Mrs Carlton. She's been trying to sell for ages and has been let down several times.'

'We're not likely to let her down.' I stroked Rollo's head. 'The survey was all in order and the solicitors are now proceeding to contract. We're both of us very thrilled. Nick, since his accident, seems more happy about me working. I think, when he was in hospital, he . . .realised lots of things.'

'I'm glad.' James's head jerked up.

'So, now,' I said, feeling my way very carefully, 'I can look for a partnership within a six-mile radius of home.'

'You'll have no trouble.' James picked up my stool, and tin of tubes and jars. 'I'll put these in your car for you.' The Renault was parked in a lane just off the towpath. We set off towards it, the dogs following, I carrying my masterpiece. 'No, you'll have no trouble,' he repeated, 'good doctors are scarce, although I have to admit that I've been extremely fortunate. I've managed to acquire a part-time partner without having to advertise. Marcus Roseveare introduced me to her—a Mrs Archibald. She's a middle-aged woman who's been working in India for the World Health Organisation. She's back living in Seftonbridge now, with her disabled father. She seems a very pleasant sort; I took to her at once.'

'Oh, good,' I said, while disappointment struck me with clouting force. Until that moment I don't think I'd realised how much I'd hoped and aspired to be James's partner. . .trust a man to look after himself. It wasn't so long ago, was it, that he'd expounded the job to me—not offered it to me, in any shape or form, but he *had* sounded me out? Since then, of course, I'd told him about my difficulties with Nick, so he might have thought that the way wasn't clear, that I wouldn't continue to work. But whatever it was, whatever he'd thought, he'd got himself fixed up. So I felt disappointed—unreasonably, perhaps, but one can't help one's feelings. 'I'm glad for you,' I averred stoutly. 'Now you won't be nearly so rushed.'

'It'll make all the difference.' He handed me my paints, and my stool, when I'd unlocked the car. I seemed to do everything in slow motion, though longing to be gone. I put the painting on the passenger seat, then turned to say goodbye. He wasn't far behind me, in fact he was close, our eyes met and locked. I dizzied and seemed to swim in a sea of deep blue. Out of it I felt him touch me, heard him say crystal-clearly, 'It would never do for you and me to work in partnership, Kate.'

'Wouldn't it?' Even saying two words seemed to rob me of breath.

He shook his head, and I knew what he meant; there

was no mistaking his meaning. The small channel of space between us became electrified. He moved away from me quickly, suddenly, and perhaps he disturbed the dogs, or perhaps the atmosphere got to them; whichever it was, they set about one another, started to snarl and fight, biting, yelping, growling, rolling in the grass. The din was horrendous, I yelled, and so did James; he pitched in and grabbed Lurcher's tail. I did the same with Rollo, then, braced well back, like two people in a tug-of-war, we managed to hold them apart, while they glared at one another, baring their teeth— the lurcher's were yellow, and fang-like, and matched his narrow eyes. We held on grimly till their hackles went down, till the two sets of teeth were once more shrouded in canine lips, till the two pairs of eyes ceased to glare, and became benign again.

James set the lurcher free first and he rushed to the river to drink. I freed Rollo and he followed suit; we held our breath as we watched them. But they were all right, standing there together, heads down, slupping water, fierce exchanges forgotten, tails swinging from side to side. Presently Rollo came back to James, and the lurcher took himself off—to his home, presumably—in the direction of the bridge. 'I wonder what made them rear up like that?' James remarked, as we stood by the car again.

'Search me,' I said. 'I'm just glad they weren't hurt; dog-fights are awful.' I stroked Rollo's smooth, hard head.

'We did all the wrong things.' James snapped on his leash. 'We should have thrown water over them—filled your jar up and chucked it over them; we could have got bitten, you know.'

'Oh, well, no harm done!'

We laughed then, couldn't help it, but more in relief than amusement, and as our laughter died James reached out and drew me close. I realised then that I had known this was bound to happen one day, and, when he tilted my chin and kissed my lips, I had known that would happen too. What I hadn't known, had no notion of, was the effect it would have on me. I was transported, lifted high on delight, crested on ecstasy. My arms went round his neck and I gave myself up to the moment, to the flaring joy of being kissed by James.

I had no idea how long we stood there, but there was no jarring back to earth. The world came back with infinite tact—the breeze rustling the reeds, the sun raying dying light into our eyes, James's arms loosening about me, his voice saying, 'Now *that* is why we could never work together.'

'Yes, I know.' My voice throbbed; I could hear it. He moved a little away.

'Physical pleasure is never worth ruining everything else for, Kate. We shall have to take care not to get involved in any more dog-fights, I think!' A glint of amusement appeared in his eyes, and his mouth curved upwards, but I couldn't laugh, couldn't joke at that point. I simply wasn't amused. I knew that what had happened *shouldn't* have happened, for we were both involved with other partners to whom we owed loyalty—we were neither of us two-timing types—but I wished he wouldn't make light of it, as though it didn't matter.

'I think the best thing we can do,' I said briskly, 'is to forget it ever happened.'

'I think so too.' He stood back for me to open the car door. As I bent to get in I turned my foot and very nearly fell. 'You *are* all right, aren't you?' He sounded concerned. I slid behind the wheel and slammed the door quickly, cutting him off.

'Oh, for heaven's sake, James. . .' and now it was my turn to look and sound amused '. . .I'm not so bowled over by a single kiss that I can't steer the car safely home!'

'Of course not. . .sorry.' And now he looked angry, and I was childishly glad. We said goodbye very civilly, and I watched him go off, striding out, Rollo at his side. He was soon out of sight, the trees hid him, but several minutes passed before I put the car into reverse and backed out of the lane.

I felt shaken to the core—shattered, in fact—I had never been so moved by a man in my life, certainly not by Nick. The thought was treason, and I hated myself for it, hated my body too, for its greedy response to James's lips and hands; it was perfectly true what he'd said. Physical pleasure wasn't worth throwing everything else to the winds. I was happy with Nick in that way—not raised to the heights, it was true, but we suited one another, and beneath it all we were friends of long standing. That counted for something. . .it counted for everything. My feelings for James were flash-in-the-pan, as his were for me. Even so, I couldn't stop thinking about him; my mind refused to oust him and I thought of him all the way back to River Road.

Nick was coming to supper. Aunt Laura was poaching a salmon—a whole one, that a grateful patient had given to Uncle John.

'How did you get on?' she asked, when I let myself into the hall. She meant my painting, of course. I pulled myself together with an effort.

'All right—I enjoyed it. It was great, actually, lovely down there in the sun.'

She watched me stow my painting equipment in the cupboard under the stairs. 'As a matter of fact,' I said, still fastening the door, 'James Masefield was down there, walking his Labrador dog.'

'Was he? Oh, that reminds me,' Aunt Laura enthused, 'your uncle and I were wondering if we'd ask him and Helen Clifford over here for a meal one evening. Nick would come, of course, and there'd be Uncle and me. I could manage six quite easily. Don't you think it's a good idea?'

I couldn't think of a worse one, the thought of it made me sweat, but as it happened I was saved from replying, for Aunt caught sight of my painting, which I'd propped up against the cupboard door. 'Why, Kate, that's lovely. . . It really is!' she stood back to get a long view. 'Does Nick know you can paint like this?'

'He's seen one or two of my efforts,' I said, 'but I don't think he's all that impressed. Nick's an architect, remember. He has a great thing about perspective and line, which I don't know much about.'

'Well, I think you're very talented.' She gave me one of her hugs, then repaired to the kitchen, closing the door to shut out the odour of fish.

Uncle John was taking surgery. I could hear the drone of his voice as I went upstairs to shower and change, and reflect, once again, on how absolutely awful it would be if Aunt Laura's plan for that sixsome dinner came to fruition. But perhaps she would change her mind.

It was as I was about to step under the shower, as my right hand went out to strip off my ring and encountered nothing but unadorned flesh and bone, that my glance travelled downwards, and I saw to my horror that my engagement ring had gone. But it can't have. . . 'It can't have!' I cried the words out loud. I turned off the shower and went into the bedroom and searched through my clothes. There was no sign of it. . .no sign at all. . .but it couldn't have disappeared. I scoured the dressing-table. . .had I laid it down? I hadn't; it wasn't there. I felt clammy, yet cold as well. Had I lost it outside? Oh, surely not. . .oh, please not that. But I might have, I could easily have done so, for just lately it had got loose—I had lost weight—and had a tendency to slip round back-to-front. Once, in the garden, when I'd picked up some leaves, it had very nearly slipped off. Nick had told me to get it made smaller. 'It's not a big job,' he'd said. So I ought to have done so, I *should* have done so, but surely it couldn't be lost. Perhaps it was in the cupboard downstairs, caught up with my painting things. I tore down there, opened the cupboard, lifted everything out. I knocked down a bucket, startling Aunt Laura, who rushed through from the kitchen.

'What on earth's going on?' She stared open-mouthed, as well she might, for I was wearing my shower-cap and very little else.

'Aunt Laura,' I gasped, 'I've lost my ring, but it may be in the car.' Grabbing a raincoat, I ran out to the garage, where I searched the car seats and floor. I looked under the dashboard, down by the steering-column, even over the garage floor. It was nearly dusk, so I trained a torch over the path to the house, but there was no ring. . .no ring. . .it was nowhere to be seen. It must be down by the river! I burst back into the house. Aunt Laura was standing transfixed in the hall, and I pushed past her to the stairs. 'I'm going down there, I'm going now—down to the river to look!'

'Oh, no, Kate, you can't. . .it's getting dark!'

'I must!' I ran upstairs, and into my bedroom, where I hastily pulled on some clothes.

My aunt came with me, still protesting. 'Please, Kate, don't go. . .you'll never find it, not in this half-light. . . wait until morning, *please*!'

'I have to go now, it has to be now. Nick will be here soon. I think I know where it might be; I *have* to go and look!'

'I want to come with you, but I can't leave the phone!'

'I know, and I'll be all right.' I was off down the stairs and out of the door, and into the garage again. I backed out the car, and prayed as I did so—please, let me find my ring. It might be where I had set up my stool, it might have come off then.

My thoughts were in turmoil all the time I was driving river-wards. What would Nick say if I'd lost it—if the ring was never found? He wouldn't be furious, because he wasn't the sort of man who reacted like that, but it wouldn't improve our relationship, and that was for certain. He'd be quietly angry and hurt that I'd not treasured the ring more—not treasured it enough to do as he'd said and get it made smaller. He'd go on and on about it, and who could possibly blame him? But it wasn't lost, it couldn't be lost, I *had* to find it—I *would* find it somewhere down on the riverbank.

I parked in the lane, the same as before, and looked there first. Then, shining the torch along the ground, I made my way to the exact spot where I'd sat and sketched. I went down on my hands and knees, then, holding the torch in one hand, I riffled through the grass with my free hand, my eyes all but on the ground. It was hard to concentrate; it was eerie down there. There were so many rustlings and sighings, and once I thought there was someone behind me, stealthily stalking, right on my heels, like the Ancient Mariner's fiend. I'm a coward where lonely places are concerned, but I forced myself to stay. I had to keep searching. . . searching and searching. . .there was still the place in the lane where the dogs had fought. I would go back there, and search all over again.

It was then that the futility of what I was doing struck me full force. It was crazy, quite crazy to be searching here in the dark. Yet I still stayed, I still looked; I wasn't quite convinced. I heard the Catholic church clock strike the hour deep in the heart of the town. It was seven o'clock, and I had been here an hour. I would have to go home. I would have to make my peace with Nick, and if the ring didn't turn up I would have to reimburse him for it. I knew what it had cost— he had told me that when he'd warned me about it being loose. Nick wasn't mean—nothing *like* mean— but he was sensibly money-conscious, and, although handing over five hundred pounds wouldn't make things right, it would appease him, and, to a certain extent, ease my state of mind.

It was possible, I supposed, that someone might have picked the ring up after I'd left this afternoon, when it was still light enough to be able to see it winking up from the grass. I felt this was unlikely, however, and I tried to remember when I had last, consciously, seen it on my hand. It had been after the dog-fight; I had seen it sparkling when I'd stroked Rollo's head. Perhaps James could throw some light on the matter—yet this, too, I felt was unlikely. I began the drive home, rehearsing what I was going to say to Nick.

It was seven-fifteen and the town was busy, revving up for evening pleasures. Students cycled in droves, cafés blazed with light, couples walked arm in arm, theatre-goers whisked by in taxies, an ambulance sirened its way through the traffic lights; I pulled up just in time.

Starting off again, I reflected that I had barely fifteen minutes to get in, and changed, before Nick was due to arrive. Should I tell him as soon as he walked in, try to get him on his own? Should I wait in the drive and intercept him, tell him outside in the dark? I felt the best way was to get it over with, so maybe I'd tell Aunt Laura that I was back after a fruitless search, then go and wait in the porch.

As I made the turn into River Road, however, I saw a car slowing at our gates. Surely he hadn't got there already! I felt my insides lurch, but as I got nearer I saw that the car was longer and sleeker than Nick's; it was a black Volvo. . .and James was behind the wheel.

Hope surged through me then, for had he found my ring? Surely he had. . .oh, surely he had. . .for why else would he have come? He saw me approaching. I turned my car with its nose inside the gates; he got out of his, and we met on the gravel, screened by the laurel hedge. And even then, upset though I was, the sight of him gladdened me. Everything will be all right now, I thought; James will sort it out.

I saw his hand go into his jacket and draw out an envelope. I could see the white of it, hear its crackle. 'James!' My voice was hoarse.

'I've come to restore lost property.' He loomed tall against the light of the street-lamp behind him, and held out the envelope.

I gasped, and took it from him. 'It's my ring, isn't it? I've been looking everywhere; I've just been——'

'I've only just found it——' he sounded aloof '—when I finished surgery.'

'Oh, I didn't mean. . . I only meant. . . Where did you find it?' His manner disconcerted me; I couldn't gauge his mood.

'At the back of my sweater, embedded in the neck, caught up in the wool.'

I stared at the blur of his face in the dark. 'Then it must have been when. . .it must have been. . .' I knew full well when it must have been. It must have been during our embrace by the river, when my arms were round his neck.

'The ring is too big for you, isn't it?' He seemed to stand taller than ever. 'It slides back to front; it was the front diamond part that dug itself into my sweater. When you brought your hand down from my neck. . .' he was being so clinical I could have died '. . .your finger must have drawn out of the hoop, leaving me with a small fortune dangling from my nape.'

Perhaps I was meant to laugh, but I couldn't manage so much as a smile. Instead I stammered, 'It—it was good of you to bring it.' I swallowed against a dry throat.

'I don't usually take, nor keep, what's not mine.' He was referring, I knew, to a great deal more than just the return of my ring.

I felt a little stir of anger then. There was no need, surely, to be quite so high and mighty, so holier-than-thou. When I heard a car coming down the road I said defensively, 'This will be Nick. I'm expecting him— he's coming to supper.'

'I'd better get off, and let him pull in.' James turned back to the gates.

'You could stay and meet him properly.'

'Another time, perhaps.'

I watched him cross the verge, glance towards Nick's car, give a little salute, then get into the Volvo. As he drove off, the porch light snapped on, and Aunt Laura came running out. 'Kate?'

'It's all right, Aunt, I've got my ring; James brought it back. He found it with. . .among his things. He's gone now and Nick's arrived.'

'Good *Lord*!' I heard her say. 'Talk about a close shave!'

I didn't answer; I was looking at Nick, who was coming across the lawn. His gait was odd, slow and stiff, as though his legs wouldn't bend. He walked towards me stumblingly, and I ran forward and grasped his arm.

'Are you all right, Nick? Are you feeling queer?' It was Aunt Laura who spoke. She took hold of his other arm and we got him into the house. It was there, collapsed on the hall chair, that he told us his dreadful news.

'Mother's died,' he said, 'two hours ago in the General Hospital.'

CHAPTER EIGHT

EVENTUALLY Nick was able to tell us exactly what had happened. By then Uncle John had finished surgery, and we were all in the sitting-room. Apparently the hospital had telephoned Nick at his office at ten a.m. to tell him that his mother had been admitted with a cerebral haemorrhage. She had been found by a neighbour, who called at the house and found her on the floor in the kitchen, beside her ironing board.

'She mentioned, at breakfast, that she'd got a lot of ironing to do,' Nick said. 'She didn't seem ill then, she was singing about the house—you know how she does . . .did, I mean. I just said goodbye and left.'

'She probably had very little warning, lad,' Uncle John put in at this point.

We had a meal—the salmon—and we all ate moderately well, even Nick, although I'm sure he didn't know what went into his mouth. Everything I ate tasted like gravel; only Uncle John relished the food. He tried to hide his enjoyment of it, but kept eyeing the new potatoes that were left in the dish so ruefully that Aunt Laura pushed them towards him. 'For goodness' sake, eat them,' she said quickly, looking guiltily at Nick.

As we drank coffee by the fire afterwards, she suggested that Nick might like to stay at the Larches for a time—at least until after the funeral. 'I would feel happier if you did, dear, and I know Kate would.' A quick glance at me confirmed this, for of course I wanted to do all I possibly could for Nick at this awful time. 'John will drive you home now, to collect your things,' she added.

I went to Park Road with them, and while Nick packed a bag I went round fastening doors and windows, and generally tidying up. I felt very odd indeed in the kitchen, folding Alma's ironing board. The iron was switched off and up-ended, so most likely she had begun to feel ill and had acted instinctively and promptly, which was like her, of course. One of Nick's shirts was on the board, and as I looked at it the fact that Alma was no longer with us became very real at last. I was still standing there, feeling peculiar, when Nick came in. Uncle John was out in the garage, turning the gas meter off.

'Once everything has been cleared up, we can live here,' Nick said, looking over at me. 'There's no point in buying another property when this one's dropped into my lap. Mother will have left everything to me— and no, I'm not being hard. It's only by talking about the future—looking forward to our life together—that I can get through this present time. Surely you can understand that?'

I could, but I was still shocked by his statement. To be thinking of benefiting from Alma's death within hours of it happening was awful. If he'd *thought* these things—and sometimes we can't help what springs to mind—he shouldn't have given them voice, not for a day or two.

It was an unreal week that followed; even the ordinary things seemed strange. Uncle and I carried on as usual with the practice work, of course. Aunt Laura took Nick under her wing, dispatching him to town on Monday morning. 'It's best for him to be occupied,' she said.

James telephoned to say how sorry he was about Alma's death. 'I saw the notice in the evening paper, Kate. What a shock for you both.'

'Yes, it was.' I was glad to hear from him, so glad to hear his voice. 'Alma died that day I was sketching by the bridge. . .you know, when Nick came to the house.'

'How has he taken it?'

'Well, naturally he's pretty shattered, but we've got him living here, with us, for the moment. Aunt Laura thought it best.'

'How will it affect your marriage plans or. . .don't you know?'

'Well, we shan't be buying the house we viewed— the one belonging to your patient. We're going to live in Alma's—it's been left to Nick, you see.'

There was a small silence, then I heard James say, 'Good idea, if you like the place.'

'We do. . .both of us. . . I've always liked it.'

My words came out in jerks. I could hear my voice cracking, and perhaps James could too, for after several more phrases that suited the occasion he said, 'Take care,' and rang off.

I was still sitting there, looking at the phone, when Doris came in to tell me she had got her hospital appointment with Mr Ford-Hobbs. She was to see him in his clinic on Maundy Thursday, the day of Alma's funeral—in other words, the day after tomorrow, which was really very quick. 'And if I have to go into hospital,' she said, though I wasn't deceived by her manner, 'my husband can cope, and so can the boys. Now, doctor, you've got fourteen patients this morning, and the district nursing sister is coming to talk to you about old Mrs Garson, the one who broke her hip.'

'Yes, all right,' I said, taking the hint, and the notes

from Doris, but I felt worried about her, as I called the first patient in.

My mother and father, who had known Alma well, travelled down from Berwick for her funeral, and at midday on Thursday she was laid to rest in the local cemetery. Most of Nick's relatives came back to the Larches, where Aunt Laura and Mother had prepared a substantial buffet meal, prefaced by bowls of hot soup. It was when most people were leaving that Nick told me he had decided to stay with his cousin Mark, and Mark's wife, at Reading for a time. 'I'm going back with them now,' he said. 'I feel I must get away. I'll ring you, of course, every day, and I won't be gone for long.'

'But Nick. . .' I stared at his cases, which he'd brought downstairs. 'It's so quick—I mean, are you sure?'

'They can take me back with them,' he said practically, 'and I knew you'd understand.'

'Yes, of course,' I heard myself say, as he kissed me, then went to say goodbye to Aunt Laura and Uncle John, and thank them for what they'd done. I didn't understand, though, not really, for, although he'd been through a lot, surely we ought to be together, surely it should be me he was needing and wanting, surely *I* should be his support? And, because none of this seemed to be the case, I felt I'd failed him. It was a bitter moment when he drove off with Mark and Estelle.

Doris arrived on her bicycle before I went back into the house. She had agreed to come in for evening surgery, as Aunt Laura would be busy. Wondering how she had got on with Mr Ford-Hobbs, I went through to the surgery quarters and she presently joined me there.

Watching her sliding buttons into my newly laundered coat, I was reminded of my ring and the way it had 'buttoned' into James's sweater. . .'A chance in a million,' I said out loud, and Doris looked up.

'What is?' Her eyes went smaller as she took her glasses off.

'Oh, nothing much, Doris, I'm talking to myself. What's more to the point, how did you get on this afternoon, with Mr Ford-Hobbs, I mean?'

'I'm being admitted next Wednesday, for an op on the Friday.' She held the coat out and I slipped my arms in it, glad to turn my back.

'Oh, well, that's good in a way, isn't it?'

'Yes, I don't mind a bit, the sooner the better, get it over. I shall be here on Tuesday, so we can discuss arrangements then. Now, Doctor,' her voice was brisk, 'here's the list for tonight.'

Taking the list from Doris, I got out the medical notes.

The first patient was Mrs Rudd, an eighty-eight-year-old woman with her right arm in plaster. She came in with her daughter. 'My mother's got a lump on her eyelid,' she explained, once they were seated.

'Oh, dear, that's a nuisance for you, Mrs Rudd.' I smiled at the old lady. Than I washed my hands and gently examined her eye. 'It's a chalzian,' I said, 'it's caused by a blockage of one of the glands that line the lid margins. It's not serious and it'll probably go away on its own. How long have you had it?'

'About a week, doctor.' Mrs Rudd blinked rapidly.

'More like three,' the daughter corrected.

'Well, you can try to help it on its way by using a hot compress. Wring a face flannel out in hot water, hold it on your eyelid, pressing towards the lashes—very gently, mind. Try that and if it still doesn't go, come back and see me again.'

It was as she got up to go that I noticed her plaster, or rather her fingers sticking out from it—they were bluish and very puffed up. 'How long has your hand been like that?' I was so startled that I snapped. 'Didn't you notice how swollen and discoloured your fingers were getting? Didn't *you* notice?' I swung round to the daughter, who bridled and looked annoyed.

'Of course, but I didn't think it was anything—just part of breaking her wrist.'

'But they must have told you, at the hospital, to watch out for this sort of thing.'

'They might have—I don't remember.' The daughter's chin went up. 'All I know is, it's been such a nuisance, she can't even dress herself. If we have to go back to Casualty, it'll mean waiting up there for hours.'

'Even so, your mother will have to go, Miss Rudd.' I put on my sternest expression. 'The plaster is too tight across the back of the hand and around the bases of the thumb. It needs cutting back, and the sooner the better. I'll give you a note to take.'

'Couldn't *you* do it, dear?' Mrs Rudd asked, as I adjusted her sling in such a way that her hand was pointing up.

'Believe me, I would if I could,' I smiled, 'but I mustn't interfere with your plaster. I haven't got the right equipment here, whereas the hospital have. They'll know exactly what to do, and all that tight swelling will go down, even as you watch it, just like a pricked balloon. It's important to go; it would be foolish to leave it, it could be serious.'

'I've got the van outside, I'll run her up now.' The daughter was a florist. She still looked huffed, but less so. She even told her mother not to worry. 'It'll be all right, Mum, we'll get it seen to,' she said, as I scribbled the note.

I saw eight other patients—five with respiratory troubles, one pregnant girl with dyspepsia, a man getting over shingles, and a little boy with an ear infection, but by half-past six I was writing up the last of the notes, and Doris was wrapping her head and half her shoulders in a woollen scarf, all ready to cycle home.

'See you on Tuesday,' she called out from the doorway.

'Yes, see you, Doris, thanks for coming.' I refrained from saying more.

'Are you covering for anyone over the weekend?' she asked.

'No, I'll be free,' I told her. And I doubt, I thought, hearing her close the back door, if I'll ever be asked to cover for James Masefield again. He and his new partner, Mrs Archibald, would work out a rota between them, in the same way as Uncle and I did. It was only when a GP was on his own that he had to rely on the good nature of his colleagues if he wanted a weekend off.

One thought led to another, and I fell to wondering when James and Helen Clifford would marry—probably quite soon. Eloise would be packed off to boarding school, so no worry about her. James had laid his plans extremely well, and they would all come to fruition. Bully for him. My Biro ran out, and I threw it into the bin.

I knew I was trying to stir up anger, even whip up a little dislike, where he was concerned, but no hate feelings came, although some of the other sort did. I thought of his kiss and the way he had held me, and then I refused to think of him one second longer. I took off my coat and went into the sitting-room.

My parents were in there, Aunt and Uncle too; they were watching Channel Four News. Families are special, they are part of oneself, they're supporters through thick and thin. Yet, that evening by the fire, probably because Nick had gone off, I felt odd man out; I felt at odds with the world.

During the next day, Good Friday, though, Mother spoke her mind. 'I think it's a good thing Nick has gone away for a time,' she said, 'for it strikes me you need a breathing space quite as much as him.'

'That's a funny thing to say!' I exclaimed.

'I could say a good deal more, but I won't because it's not my business, you must sort it out for yourself. Anyway, I'm glad he's gone; your father and I want to see something of you for the short time we're here.' Having said this, she took the spring flowers she had picked earlier on, into the kitchen and arranged them in a vase. By the way she spoke, and by the way she thrust those innocent blooms into place, I knew she suspected I was feeling unhappy and blamed Nick for it. This wasn't entirely fair, of course, but nevertheless I had to admit it was good and comforting to have her on my side.

On Saturday Father drove us into the town to do the shopping for Aunt Laura, and, on coming out of Boots, who should we run into but James and Helen Clifford. Eloise was between them, in her red coat, holding her father's hand.

It was nine days since I'd seen James, and so much had happened since then. Hoping that my instant flutters didn't show, I introduced my parents. I sensed

Mother's interest in James—she looked at him over-long, then bent down to Eloise and admired her baby doll.

'She should have outgrown dolls by now, don't you think?' Helen's voice was sharp.

'No, I don't, Miss Clifford,' Mother straightened up, 'Kate wasn't weaned from dolls till she was going on nine years old. Children shouldn't grow up too soon; childhood's a magic time.'

'I agree,' James sided with her. I could see they liked one another. I was proud of Mother; she looked willowy lean in her black and white houndstooth suit, her hair like burnished copper wound round her head in a pleat. James looked from one to the other of us. 'You're so like your mother, Kate, that I couldn't possibly, not possibly, have failed to guess who she was.'

'People often say that,' Mother laughed, tilting back her head, 'but at least,' she went on, 'you don't spoil things by adding that fatuous comment about us looking like sisters, making Kate feel fifty-plus and me pleased, but slightly patronised.'

The three of us laughed. Father and Helen were having a tête-à-tête conversation a little apart from us. 'I suppose you came to Seftonbridge for the funeral,' I heard Helen say. 'Do you live far from here?'

'Yes, we do, at Berwick-on-Tweed; my wife is a Borderer,' Father said with beaming pride, then went on to explain that their next trip would would be a happy family occasion. . .'For Kate's wedding, you know. I love a wedding. We're looking forward to it, aren't we, dear?' He smiled at Mother, who confirmed that they were. 'It'll be an occasion to remember——' he was all but rubbing his hands '—our son and his wife from New Zealand are coming over for it. Tom, Nick and Kate used to play together as children. Nick's practically one of the family already. . .just needs to tie the knot.'

'When is the knot-tying to be?' Helen turned her face to me.

'We haven't settled on a date,' I told her. 'Mrs Carrington's death has made us re-jig our plans.' I deplored the turn the conversation had taken, and stared down at Eloise.

'Life has been tough on your fiancé recently.' James's comment dropped into the little silence that followed; I made myself meet his gaze.

'He'd have been lost without Kate,' Father was saying, just as I was approached by a woman in a trailing mackintosh, a headscarf binding her hair. I felt a shoot of alarm, for I knew her, recognised her at once. She was Mrs Carlton, the vendor of the house at Cletford Road. She meant business too, in the unpleasant sense—I could tell that by her face, and by the way she literally thrust herself in front of Father and Helen, to confront me close to; I willed myself not to step back.

'You're the young woman who was buying my house, who promised to buy my house. . .promised, promised . . .there'd be no let-down, that's what you said! Now I've heard. . .my solicitor has told me. . .that you're backing out of it! You and your boyfriend *guaranteed* that you'd complete within a few weeks. I suppose you've found somewhere you like better. Well, I've heard all that before, and let me tell you——'

'Mrs Carlton. . .' I managed to speak at last, aware as I did so of Father bristling behind her, of Mother gripping my arm, of passers-by looking curiously at us, of James stirring at my side. 'Perhaps,' I said, as icily as I could muster, 'it's not been explained to you that——'

'Oh, excuses, explanations, reasons. . .don't bore me with those! There are always those, always something; the plain fact is that you've gone back on what you said, and I've been let down again. People like you should be fined, should be prosecuted, should be taken to court!'

'Now, look here. . .' Father shouted and moved forward, but James was quicker and more controlled; he touched Mrs Carlton's arm just enough to move her away from me. She swung round on him; she was a tall woman and her mac slapped against my legs.

'Why. . . Dr Masefield!' She was clearly astonished to find him there. She'd had eyes for no one but me, her quarry, when she'd leapt out through Boots' glass doors.

'Good morning, Mrs Carlton.' He was her doctor, I remembered, and the smile he gave her would have calmed a herd of charging buffaloes, let alone one irate woman. 'I happen to know,' he continued smoothly, 'that Dr Chalmers, here, liked your house, so did her fiancé; they wanted to buy it, but there has been a sudden bereavement in the family, which has drastically altered their plans. Having said that, I'm sure you'll soon sell; you have a very attractive property, and you've kept it in ace condition, which always counts when one wants to sell.'

'I didn't know *you* were a doctor,' she said, turning round to me again. Evidently being a GP covered a multitude of sins, for her expression now was admiring, even deferential, embarrassing me far more than her former fierce one had done. 'Not knowing all the facts,

I was justly angry.' She smiled, showing a rim of gum as well as white, strong teeth. 'If I've upset you, I'm sorry.' Her smile swept all of of us, even Helen, who looked amused, then off she went, striding off like a man.

'Well, *really*!' Father turned to look after her, Mother raised her eyebrows at James, and put an arm round my shoulders. 'What a vituperative woman!' she exploded. 'Nick should have dealt with her, gone to see her, not left it to the lawyers.'

'Nick has had enough to do,' I said shortly, 'but thank you very much——' I was looking at James '—for taking my part. She *was* a bit fierce!'

He laughed but looked thoughtful, and I felt he was about to comment on this, but Mother was bent on praising him. 'You were splendid,' she said, 'you defused a very sparky situation.'

'James has that tendency,' Helen said drily, while I, nudging Mother, suggested that we ought to get going or we'd never get the shopping done.

'You're right, darling. Saturday shopping is murder.' She smiled dazzlingly at James, who had the look of a man who would have thrown down his coat for her to walk on. He shook hands with both my parents. Helen looked bored, while Eloise, delighted that she needn't stand still for one second longer, ducked her head and led the way into the shop.

'Pretty woman, Dr Masefield's girl,' Father eulogised over Helen.

'Pretty as Dresden china, and as hard,' Mother declared sweetly, as we dived into Sainsbury's, leaving Father outside. 'Are she and James engaged, Kate, or are they just. . .?'

'Most likely both.' We stopped in front of a wall of yoghurts, of all varieties; I saw them through a haze.

'He's attractive, the gallant type, and the little girl is enchanting. What happened to his wife?' I told her. 'Oh, dear, how sad,' she said. 'Of course the child needs a mother. What does the Clifford girl do?'

'She's a dental surgeon.' I watched Mother throw a tub of margarine into the basket.

'That I can believe!' She pulled a face. 'I can see her wielding a drill. She got that kind of look about her—concentrated and relentless. How does he—James, I mean—get on with Nick?'

'They've never actually been introduced, only sighted one another,' I said. 'James isn't Nick's doctor and they've never met socially.'

Mother looked surprised. 'But I thought you all met up at the Roseveares' party. I'm sure John told me. . .'

'That's true,' I said, 'but Nick didn't come; he was ill so had to cry off.'

'It seems to me——' Mother gave me a look '—that Nick cries off from all sorts of things. I suppose——' she inspected a packet of sausages, then put them back on the rack '—I suppose you *are* in love with him. . . you're not just making do?'

'That's an odd thing to say!' I snapped back, for it was as though she had touched on a nerve.

'OK, then, forget it, sorry I said that.' She smiled an apology, and the rest of the shopping was done with only the usual small talk about brands and prices, much to my relief.

CHAPTER NINE

NICK telephoned me each evening during Easter. He was feeling better, he said. 'It made sense to get away, Kate, just for a little while.' I agreed with him, for perhaps he was right, and perhaps I'd been silly to resent him flying off, as he had, so quickly after the funeral. However, when he rang me on Tuesday morning, from his office in town, I had a job not to explode when he blithely informed me that he was staying with Mark and Estelle for another ten days. 'I can commute from Reading quite easily,' he went on, 'so there's no reason why not.'

'None at all,' I said, but I doubt if he took the comment as I meant it, for he went on chatting much as usual and only left off when I said I was in the middle of surgery, and that life had to go on. So, yes, I did feel angry at first, but then I took to wondering if Nick might be dreading returning to the Park Road house. If he was, it was understandable, but, even so, he couldn't stay away forever, and, as we intended to *live* in the house once we were married, the situation had to be faced. It was no good putting it off.

It was Doris's last morning before she went into hospital, so that, too, was trying, for she naturally felt on edge. Wishing her luck and promising to visit her on Wednesday evening, I watched her wind herself in her scarves and pedal off down the drive.

After lunch I drove Mother and Dad to the station and put them on the London train. Then, as I drove back through the town, I saw the traffic diversion and heard the pom-pom-pom-pom of Seftonbridge's town band. Of course, the parade, the hospital parade, I'd forgotten all about it. Feeling rather guilty for, after all, I ought to support it, I left the car meter-parked and went to choose my viewing point which, as I was close, was the top of Bateman Street. There were people lining the pavement, but the crowds weren't so thick as they would have been in the High Street, and I'd be able to see quite well.

The sound of the band was getting closer, playing 'A Life on the Ocean Wave' as it swung round the War Memorial, the drum major strutting in front. The sun glinted on their brass instruments, and the first of the floats—a naval scene—was well received by the crowd.

As the tune change to 'Crown Imperial', a historical scenario passed. Undergraduates brought round collecting tins, and, moving to unzip my bag, I saw a little girl in a blue jumpsuit sitting high on a man's shoulders—her father's shoulders, moreover, for the child was Eloise. Her hands were on his head—on his thick, dark hair—*his* hands grasped her legs. As my vision unblurred, I looked again. Mrs Shinway was there too, while behind them, on the steps of Gregson's, the dental surgeons, was Helen Clifford— fair-haired and professional, poised there in her white coat.

They hadn't seen me, and I didn't want them to. Thump. . .thump. . .thump. . .the band was playing 'Colonel Bogey', while a coach and four, with bewigged ladies peeping out of its windows, rolled past amid much applause. I tried my best to move further away from the group near Gregson's, for I was in no mood to make stilted conversation, which was the only sort I could ever manage to get past my lips when Helen was about.

The parade continued to drool past, we had nearly seen it all. It would pass into Station Road next, then left into Barrington Street. Behind the last float, which was just beginning to pass Gregson's windows, was a black stallion with a Knight in Shining Armour on his back. It brought forth cheers from the crowd, and perhaps it was this, coupled with the sound of a car backfiring, that made the stallion rear in fright, eyes rolling, ears back, front hooves flailing the air. It skittered sideways on to the pavement, its rider struggling to gain control. The crowd screamed and scattered, fell back in a wave. I was knocked off my feet. Amidst more screams I managed to get up, rolling over on to my knees just in time to see the horse back in the road, cantering past with something underneath it. . . something caught, entangled in its hooves. . . *a child in a buggy!* Then, in a flash of white, there was something else. . .someone else under there. . .unbuckling, snatching, pulling free. . .falling back on to the pavement with the baby on top of her. . . The crowd closed in, but not before I had seen that the girl, the rescuer, was Helen. I pushed and tried to reach her, but James was first, breaking through from the other side. 'Move, please. . .out of the way!' His voice held authority. people parted in a wave, and I saw Helen handing the yelling baby to a girl who was plainly its mother, who was crying and hugging it. Helen just stood there, her coat dirtied, her hair all over the place. James took her by the arm, then, as she stumbled, lifted her bodily. I followed as best I could, for people were crowding again.

I guessed James was taking Helen to her flat, which

seemed to be the case, for as they got to Gregson's I saw that he was setting her down on her feet. They began to mount the steps, he holding her tightly against him. I called out, 'Is she all right?' and they both turned round, while Eloise, standing near, held back by Mrs Shinway, yelled my name, and tried to get to me.

'Kate! Where have you sprung from?' James' flippant tone hid a deep concern, I could see that.

'Is Miss Clifford all right?' I asked.

'I think so, yes, I'm getting her inside.'

Helen spoke then, for the first time. 'For heaven's sake stop talking about me as though I'm deaf and blind! I'm perfectly all right, just shaken, that's all, there's no need for all this fuss!' It helped her to be angry, I could see that, even understand it. 'I was brought up with horses,' she said more quietly, 'and I've never been scared of them, nor them of me—even that gorgeous beast.' Her eyes moved over my shoulder and, turning round, I saw that the now becalmed horse was being ridden away.

'Well, if you're sure there's nothing I can do,' I said, still stuck at the foot of the steps.

'There isn't, Kate, thanks—' James glanced at me, as he eased Helen through the doors '—but perhaps you could ask Maud Shinway to take Lou home. Tell her to get a taxi, not wait around for a bus.'

'I'll do better than that, I'll drive them,' I said, thankful that I could do *something*. I pushed through to them; the crowd was dispersing, no one had been injured. The only damage was to the buggy, but even that was capable of being pushed home, the baby inside it tear-stained like his young mother, but otherwise all right.

All the way home Mrs Shinway kept on about how

brave Helen had been. 'I would never have believed it, Doctor. . .never have thought she'd got it in her. She never gives me the feeling that she's fond of kiddies. And she risked her life, didn't she?'

'Yes,' I said, for there was no disputing it.

'She was so quick!'

'Yes, she was.'

'Will Daddy be long, do you think?' Eloise piped up from the back.

'He'll be home for tea, I'm quite sure,' Mrs Shinway told her. 'Now, thank Dr Kate for bringing us home,' she said a few minutes later, as I turned the car into Theodore Road.

She did so, and when I let her out she gave me a kiss as well. 'See you,' she called, running up the path—a small sprite in blue. She was, as Mother said, an enchanting child, but it was of her father I was thinking as I drove swiftly home. I wished I could have been the one to do a brave act like Helen, right under his gaze too, and have him look after me. I could still see them going up those steps, his arm wrapped round her, her fair hair blowing up over the side of his face.

He rang me after evening surgery to thank me for bringing Eloise and Mrs Shinway home safely out of the scrum. 'Oh, that's all right,' I assured him. 'I'm just glad I could help. I never meant to watch the parade, you know. I'd forgotten all about it. I'd just taken Mother and Dad to the station, and it wasn't until I heard the band and saw the traffic diversion that the penny finally dropped.'

'I should imagine that, fund-wise, the hospital did very well,' he said. 'I've never seen such crowds. In the High Street, where we made for first, they were standing ten deep, and still coming in.'

'Miss Clifford *is* all right, isn't she?' I felt I had to ask that.

'Absolutely fine. After half an hour she was back to normal. When I left she was treating a patient. It takes a lot to upset Helen.'

'It was brave, what she did.'

'She's modest about it, says it was a snap reaction. Standing where she was, on Gregson's steps, she was able to see the whole thing the second it happened, and then she just took off. I hadn't a clue, I just saw the horse rear, then heard the mother yell.'

'I was knocked flying, so saw it all through a forest of legs!'

'Good lord, were you hurt?' It was gratifying to hear the concern in his voice.

'Not by so much as a scratch,' I laughed, 'but I'm keeping away from hospital parades in future. . .they'll get my donations by post!'

Aunt Laura came in at that point, and we concluded our conversation with the usual banal leaving-off remarks. Still, I thought, putting down the receiver, he *had* telephoned, but then he would always do the right thing, he was that sort of man.

Doris, when I went to see her next evening, was outwardly calm, sitting up in bed in Carter Ward. 'I feel better now I'm *in* here,' she said. Her husband, Ron, was the fidgety one; he couldn't hide his nerves. He left when I did, asking me questions, wanting to be reassured.

'Even if it's what we think it is, she'll be all right,' won't she?' he whispered to me in the lift.

I knew that the surgeons were all but certain that Doris's lump was malignant. I recalled Mr Ford-Hobbs' words to me on the phone the other night. 'At Mrs

Leigh's age, a craggy lump always gives rise to concern. However, the fact that it's free-moving *is* a good sign.'

I clung to this—to the last part, I mean—when I answered Ron. 'Doris is in the best possible hands, and I feel very optimistic.' This wasn't an anxiety-relieving lie, either, for I *was* optimistic, in spite of Uncle John's air of gloom, which had grains of selfishness in it:

'She's a first-class receptionist, we'll have a job to replace her,' he'd said, and my aunt had told him off.

However, there was no need to telephone the ward to ask how she was on Thursday, for Ron came to the house at lunchtime to tell Uncle and me that frozen section had found Doris's lump to be benign. Uncle rang Mr Ford-Hobbs and learned that they had found a fibroidoma, which had been excised, and Doris still had her breast.

As it happened I was at the hospital next day, Friday, as Uncle wanted me to attend a film show there, on cardio-vascular disease. 'It's being put on by Professor Ingram,' he said, 'he's a very eminent man. I'd go myself, but I've half a dozen house-calls to make. Anyway, here's the invitation.' He handed me the card. 'You can tell me about it this evening after surgery.'

I set off at two-thirty, and, bearing in mind that there might be quite a crowd attending, and parking space might be scarce, I travelled there by bus.

After a quick run up to the ward to see Doris, who had Ron with her again, I made my way to the old boardroom, where the slides were to be shown. I found it packed with people—the majority of them men, standing around, talking in groups; there were rows of chairs at one end. I was given a name badge by a young clerk, who stuck it on my jacket, labelling me 'Dr John Chalmers'. 'I hope you don't mind,' she said.

I assured her I didn't, not in the least. . .'I'm here in my uncle's stead.' After all, what's in a name? I thought, going forward to speak to another woman doctor who was standing on her own.

'What a crowd,' she said. 'I hope there are going to be enough chairs to go round.'

She smiled at me; she was small and dark, probably in her fifties. 'However, I don't mind the floor, if not. It won't be the first time for me. I've been living in India, working for the World Health Organisation.'

Even before I glanced at her name badge, I guessed who she was—Dr Clare Archibald, James's new partner. I introduced myself, saying that I knew him, and asking how she was settling in.

'Just fine,' she enthused, 'it's so wonderful to be back in England. I feel settled already. You know how it is when something is right for you—you roll into the niche, find it fits round you, you don't have any doubts.'

I nodded, for I *did* know. I knew what she was talking about. I'd felt like that, exactly like that, when I'd joined Uncle John. But my job, of course, was temporary, whereas hers was permanent. I envied her, on several counts. She had herself organised.

When we were asked to take our seats, we naturally sat down together. It was then that she told me she was only there for the first half of the proceedings. 'Dr Masefield is coming for the second half, so he'll be able to have my seat.'

I felt a little dart of alarm-cum-pleasure that the mention of James's name always seemed to bring about and was difficult to hide. The feeling became a positive sunburst. He was coming here today. . .was actually coming. . .would soon be here! With all my heart I wished I were wearing something rather more fetching

than a sweater and skirt under my old husky jacket that
had seen better days.

'I'm sorry you can't stay for the whole of the time,' I
remarked politely to Clare Archibald, who was diving
down for her pen.

'Ah, well, duty calls, you know how it is.'

Good old duty, I thought. . . James will soon be
here. Meantime we were being silenced by a little
gnome-like man, who introduced himself as Professor
Ingram, and mounted the improvised dais.

The slides covered a wide range of cardiac diseases.
Clare Archibald took notes, I could see her scribbling,
head bent over her notebook. 'What a superb lecturer!'
she enthused, as the first half ended, and the professor
stepped down for a well-earned cup of tea.

Trays were brought round for the audience, and I
sipped mine thirstily. For the time of year the atmosphere was humid, and it was over-hot in that crowded
room; many people were stripping off coats.

James arrived when Clare Archibald and I were
discussing the possible advantages of a health centre
which the powers-that-be were proposing for
Seftonbridge. I was facing the doors, so saw him first.
'Dr Masefield has just come in,' I said, and was proud
of the nonchalance in my voice.

'Right, then, this is where I bow out.' Clare got up
and waved, indicating her seat to James, who
approached us at once—tall, dark, and apologetic as he
trod on someone's toes. He looked surprised to see
me—in fact, he halted a short way away—then came
forward, staring!.

'I was expecting Dr John!' The way he said this was
nearly accusing. Of course he might not have meant it

that way, but it left me with a feeling that he wasn't best pleased.

'He meant to come,' I told him steadily, 'but he had several house-calls to make.'

'I expect it's this flu outbreak.' He was helping Clare on with her coat.

'That's exactly what it is,' I replied, as she said goodbye and went off.

Several people came to speak to James, and he didn't sit down at once. Because of his attitude, I was tempted to tell him that he didn't *have* to remain at my side. He could swap seats with someone else, and I was just about to suggest this when he dropped down beside me, brushing my shoulder, arranging his long legs in front. 'Are you finding the slides interesting, Kate?' He turned his face to me.

'Very,' I said, not daring to move by so much as an inch. Being at close quarters was enslavement again. Even so, talking about medical matters soon brought me back to earth, and I found I could give a good account of what had been shown so far. 'We've got cor pulmonale, mitral stenosis, and endocarditis to come,' I finished, just as the lights dipped, and Professor Ingram's smooth golden-syrup voice introduced the next set of slides. They were rather more 'in-depth' than the first ones, and my interest in them was keen, but not for one moment. . .not for a single second. . . could I forget who was by my side. Every movement of his hand, every shift of his legs, impinged on my consciousness. I was with him. . .he was really here. . . even though in demeanour he was miles away, concentrating solely on what was being said from the platform. I made myself do the same.

As we were filing to the doors afterwards, he asked

me if I'd brought my car. I told him I hadn't. 'I wasn't sure about parking space,' I said.

'In that case, let me run you home. I owe you, remember!' He grinned at me, almost boyishly.

'You don't have to pay your debts. There's a bus stop right outside the gates.' I laughed back at him.

'You'll be soaked, even getting that far.' We had reached the portico, and I was amazed to see that it was not only raining, but pitching down in rivers, splashing up from the ground.

People were either turning back or turning up coat-collars, or unfurling umbrellas, making a dash for the car-parking area. 'Wait here, Kate. I'll bring the car round. At least one of us will be dry.' James went off with ducked head, just as a crowd of hospital staff charged up the steps, shrieking and laughing, rustling showerproof macs. One of them I instantly recognised, as she did me.

'Jane Aveling!' I cried, for that was who it was—the girl who had run Nick down that dreadful night in February, when the rain had been laced with ice.

'Dr Chalmers!' She looked covered in confusion, but otherwise just the same—tiny and bedraggled, her pointed face curtained by wet dark hair. 'I'm working here now,' she explained, 'I'm in the main typing pool.' She mentioned Nick; she had seen the notice of Alma's death in the paper. 'I was very sorry.' She moved her wet hair back.

'Yes, it was a shock. Nick's away at the moment, staying with a cousin in Reading,' I added, just as James's Volvo eased to a halt at the foot of the steps, and I took my leave of her.

I made a dramatic entry into his car, for as he opened the passenger door there was a flash of lightning so

sharp that I flinched, followed by a clap of thunder that
sounded as though the heavens were bursting apart. 'I
hate storms. . . I hate them!' I heard myself cry,
tumbling in beside him.

'This one's right overhead. I'll pull off the precinct
and into the Close. I can't drive through this.' He
looked unalarmed, not even mildly fazed. Didn't he, I
wondered, ever panic? Wasn't he ever afraid? Helen
was brave too. . .remember that. . .she wouldn't be
afraid in a storm. I was; I hated it, and my head began
to ache. The roar of the rain was all about us; there was
no visibility. Low clouds of greyish-yellow blocked out
the sky, then parted and broke, as the lightning flashed
. . .again. . .and again. . .and again. The air moving
outside the car was surely charged with demons, with
powerful forces trying to get in.

I have no idea how James managed to drive through
the hospital gates, then turn right into Grafton Close,
the quiet cul-de-sac where several of the more eminent
consultants had their consulting rooms. But the car
stopped, so I knew we were there; he had pulled into
the kerb. And there we sat cocooned from, yet
marooned by, a vortex of elements bent on destruction.
Even my knees shook with fear.

'Oh, Kate, Kate. . .come here, do!' James drew me
to him, pressing my head into the hollow of his
shoulder. 'It'll soon be over, you know. Inside a car is
one of the safest places to be in a storm.'

He could be calming as well as disturbing, I found.
He could soothe as well as excite. His throat was very
near my forehead, I could smell the faint tang of his
skin. I felt close to him, I felt warm and snug. I felt
perfectly safe. I lay on his shirt; half his jacket was
round me. He had pulled it round on purpose to

comfort and shield me; he'd not scoffed at my fears.
What I feel for him isn't just sexual attraction. . .this
thought came into my mind like a spinning-top, and
quick as a flash I whipped it out again. Whatever I
thought or felt, he couldn't be mine in any sense. I
knew that and I wouldn't steal him, not when the storm
was over, but while it was on. . .while it was on. . .he
was mine for a little while.

It was over in minutes. The rain ceased, turned itself
off like a tap. The clouds rolled back to show a blue
sky, a bright westering sun took the place of spiteful
lightning; it slanted into our eyes. 'Well, there you are.'
James shifted a little. 'What did I tell you?'

'All the right things.' I eased myself upright, squint-
ing in the sun.

'Sweet Kate!' His long fingers folded themselves
around mine. They encountered my ring, which glinted
up at us, its gold band obscured by sticking plaster, to
make it smaller, till I got it to a jeweller.

'Thank you for looking after me,' I said, as he let go
of my hand.

'You sound like a grateful patient.' He was fastening
his belt and I couldn't see his face—at least fully.

'That's not what I feel like,' I jerked out.

He looked at me then, and I at him, and just for a
second a different lightning forked between us, while
the thunder that followed was the sound of my own
heartbeats in my ears.

A pipping horn behind us broke the spell, and
galvanised James into switching on the ignition and
moving away from the kerb. 'Interlude over,' I heard
him say, as he drove through a lake of water into the
road centre and turned left into Princes Parade.

I rolled down the window, the air rushed in, sweetly

clean and fresh. On our right the towers and pinnacles of St Saviour's college and Chapel reared palely cream against a rain-washed sky. Ought I to be marrying Nick when I felt as I did about James? Was it right to do so . . .was it fair to him. . .*was it fair to myself*? Of course it is, I told myself stoutly. Nick is the one I want, have always wanted. James is just. . .a new experience. And even as I thought that last profane thought—for that was what it was—I denied it. I just didn't dare examine how much he meant to me.

All this wrangle in my mind kept me silent, and I felt James glance at me once or twice. Then, as we were crossing Garrod's Bridge, he said in level tones, 'You don't need to worry, Kate. Nothing important happened. You haven't broken any laws, or vows, nor overstepped the mark by allowing yourself to be consoled while the storm raged overhead.'

'Thank you for pointing that out to me.' I tried to smile and failed.

'It seemed to be necessary.' He passed a van. 'When are you expecting Nick back?'

'Sunday week.'

'Oh, not long now.'

'No, not long now.' I couldn't seem to be able to get my tongue down from the roof of my mouth.

'And you haven't got all that hassle of looking for a house.'

'No, that's true, and I like Alma's house.' I felt I had to add this for good measure, and to make him see that I hadn't any doubts. Yet you're full of them, aren't you . . .full of doubts? my inner voice was saying. And each day another one makes itself felt. . . You ought to heed them, you know.

James got out and opened the door for me when we

reached the Larches. Apart from anything else, he was
the most courteous man I had ever met in my life.
'Good luck, Kate,' he said, touching my face, and then
he was back in the car, and reversing, and turning, and
driving off down the road.

CHAPTER TEN

I RAN into Clare Archibald again on the following Thursday, when she told me that consternation was reigning at Theodore Road, due to Rollo's disappearing at breakfast-time, and not coming back.

'Oh, dear! Still, him being a male,' I said, 'and it being spring-time too!'

'Oh, quite,' she said and laughed a little, 'and I'm sure he'll come back all right, but naturally enough the child is upset, and so are the Shinways and James.'

'Yes, Eloise adores the dog.' My mind slipped back to that morning in mid-February, when she had wanted to take Rollo to Lewes to see her grandparents. I also remembered her joyful reunion with him on her return, and the way she had looked after him at her party, making sure that he came to no harm. 'Well, I hope he turns up,' I said quickly, taking my leave of Clare. She was just coming out of the hospital as I was going in. I was on my way to collect Doris, who was being discharged, and as her husband's van was in for repair I had said I would run her home.

Up in Carter Ward I found her saying goodbye to the other patients, going from bed to bed, like Royalty, having a word with each one. 'It's super to be going home,' she said on our way out to the lifts, 'but I almost feel guilty at walking out and leaving them still there. You get to know people very quickly in hospital, Doctor, and you hear all about their families, and troubles, and everything. That woman you saw in a blue bedjacket has just had a mastectomy. She doesn't seem to mind, but she's not married, so perhaps that makes a difference. The woman on the other side of her is practically stone deaf; the nurses had to write everything down for her, or show her diagrams. She's got cataracts as well, so can't lipread, at least not very well. She's in for a lumpectomy as I was, but is having some tests done first. I mean to pop up and see them all when I'm in Outpatients next week. That's when I'm having my stitches out. After that I can come back to work.'

'Not for another three weeks at least,' I told her firmly. 'You need time to get over all the worry and stress, and Aunt Laura is managing. . .after a fashion,' I remembered to add, for this was one of the times when Doris needed to feel she was indispensable.

She chattered away in true Doris fashion as I drove through the town. It was futile, of course, but now and again I found myself looking out for a big cream Labrador ambling along by himself. I actually saw two exactly like Rollo, but they were both on leads held, presumably, by someone entitled to be in charge of them. Rollo would be anxious to return home eventually, I was sure; all I hoped was that his wanderings hadn't taken him into the traffic zone.

Next day, Friday, my day off, I rang Mrs Shinway during the morning, to ask if the prodigal had returned. She sounded hoarse and unlike herself, as though she had a cold, and no, the dog wasn't back, she said. 'We're notifying the police, not that they're likely to do much, Doctor; they're busy people, aren't they? It's Eloise I'm worried about; she's refusing to eat.' There was the sound of coughing at the other end, then Mrs

Shinway saying that she'd have to go, there was someone at the door.

'I feel very sorry for them all,' I said, going through
to Aunt Laura, who was clearing up after morning
surgery.

'Yes, well, there's nothing you can do.' My aunt
looked a little fussed. 'Kate, love, I know this is your
day off, but could you help me with these?' She meant
with a pile of filing Uncle had turfed out of his drawers.

'Yes,' I said, 'of course I will.' I was only too glad to
have something to concentrate on. It was silly to mind
so much about the happenings at Theodore Road, but
there was no denying the fact that I did, and I felt for
Eloise.

After lunch I decided to do some gardening, and I
was still outside, digging Irish peat into the borders, at
half-past five when Uncle's car eased into the garage
sweep. He came swiftly over to me. 'I've just seen
James,' he said, 'he was coming out of the police
station, shockingly worried, poor chap.'

'You mean about the dog. Mrs Shinway said——'

'I mean about Eloise—she's been missisng for over
two hours, Kate. . .since just after three o'clock.'

'*What*?' I swung round, dropping my spade, staring
at Uncle aghast.

'She was playing in the drive after she and Mrs
Shinway got back from shopping. Mrs Shinway, apparently, wasn't feeling too well, she went into the house
to sit down for a few minutes—her legs went useless.
Sounds like flu to me. Anyway, when she went out
again, there was no sign of Eloise. James was out seeing
patients. You can imagine how Maud Shinway felt.'

I was imagining how James was feeling, yet two hours
wasn't long. Eloise had almost certainly gone off to

look for her dog; she had seized her chance and made off while Mrs S. was having a rest. She was probably on her way home now; she was a sensible little girl. But two hours. . .two hours *was* long. . .a child on her own, a child of only seven years old might be in terrible danger. 'She can't be out of the area,' I was almost insisting now, 'she can't be. . .she can't be far away!'

Uncle said nothing, but I caught his expression, and I felt my blood run cold. I turned to the house, beginning to run. 'I'm going to Theodore Road,' I cried, 'there may be something I can do.' Snatching an anorak off the pegs in the hall, getting my car keys out of my bag, I made for the garage; Uncle moved the Rover so that I could get past.

The town was choked with rush-hour traffic, and I had a job to make any speed. It was six o'clock, a fine evening, but dull, and in two hours it would be dark. But Eloise would be home by then; she might even be at home now. If she wasn't, would the police be making enquiries, or would they wait till tomorrow? Two hours, nearly three now, wasn't all that long, but a child missing was always treated with the utmost seriousness. Almost certainly Eloise had gone out to look for Rollo and got lost, or got shut in somewhere, or had fallen and hurt herself, perhaps sprained her ankle. My mind was refusing to admit the possibility that she could have been harmed. . . I wouldn't think that. . . I would *not* think it. . .but thoughts are hard to control in nightmare situations. All I knew was my heart bled for James.

There was a police car outside his gate when I turned into Theodore Road. Clare Archibald was taking surgery and I walked into the waiting-room, through into the living part of the house without so much as knock-

ing—knocking didn't matter, there was no time for it—
all that mattered was getting to James.

He was talking to two uniformed police officers, who
were sitting on the settee, one at each end of it, one of
them taking notes. He was giving them a photograph of
Eloise, and it looked as though they were just about to
take their leave, for they got up as I burst in. James
introduced me—'A colleague of mine, Dr Kate
Chalmers'—then, asking me to sit down, he took the
two officers to the door. I heard the car drive off, then
he came back in. 'It's good of you to come.'

'That's all right.' I didn't know what else to say. I
was shocked by his appearance; every line on his face
looked scored.

'I've been to every house in the road,' he told me,
'checked with all her friends, checked garages and
sheds, an empty house four doors down from here. I've
been down to the river, all along by the bridge, and
down to the swimming enclosure, in case she'd got
herself shut in one of the huts. I went along to the
school, rang the hospital. It was on my way back from
there that I called in and told the police.' He recited all
this tonelessly, didn't falter once, but his eyes were
haunted, and it hurt me to look at them.

'Three hours isn't all that long, James——' oh, how
could my voice be so steady? '—and I know you're
going to tell me that it feels like eternity, but actually,
you know, it *is* only a very short while. Eloise will come
back, or be brought back, any time now.'

He was pacing the room; I was on my feet, for to
stay sitting down seemed all wrong. To stand was
better, for it fostered the feeling that we were ready for
anything.

'What worries me, Kate——' he went to the window

and stood there looking out '—what worries me is my firm conviction that she wouldn't wander off. Not even to try to find Rollo would she go further than out of this road. She has been told, warned seriously about going off on her own. She's a sensible, biddable little girl, and she keeps her promises.'

I joined him at the window. I put my hand through his arm; he pressed it to his side and I felt the terrible tension in him. It was as we stood there, staring out at the neat front garden, that he voiced his fear, which was the same as mine had been as I'd been driving along. 'I think she's been abducted—snatched from our drive,' he said.

'Oh, no, James. . . I don't believe that!' It was necessary to lie, or I felt it was, but whether I sounded convincing I had no idea. Six-thirty chimed; in an hour it would be dusk.

'I feel I should still be searching, helping the police. Staying here, waiting for news and doing nothing, is agony.'

'Yes, I know. . . I do know.' We stared at one another. He hadn't repulsed me, thank goodness. He was letting me see his fears and share them. He was glad I was here—so far as he could be glad about anything, on this terrible, terrible evening. I longed to help him, longed to ease him, and I tried to do so with words. 'She'll be found,' I said steadily, 'and she'll be all right. I'm quite sure she will.' My hand tightened on his arm, and I felt a faint response. The clock was ticking, oh, so loudly. . .tick, tick, tick. . .such a fussy clock, such a maddening sound. 'The police——' James cleared his throat '—won't be able to do much after dark—there's so little time left now. I want to go out

there and look myself, go out there and call her
name. . .'

The phone rang, cutting off his words, and we both
spun round as though shot. James was out of the open
door and into the hall in a flash, and I followed him,
half stumbling over a mat. As he lifted the receiver I
began to pray—let it be good news, please, please let it
be good news—but as he started to speak I realised it
was no news at all, just someone, a friend, enquiring. I
saw James move a hand over his face, I heard the
controlled politeness in his voice as he said, 'Yes, very
worrying. . .yes, early yet, of course. I'm sure you're
right. Thank you for ringing. Yes, do that. . .thank
you, goodbye.' He replaced the receiver very softly and
carefully, his face a greyish white. 'That was Helen's
partner, Jeremy Gregson. He'd heard about Eloise
from his daughter; she's a secretary at Police HQ.

'Does Miss Clifford. . .does Helen know?' I asked.
'Probably she——'

'Helen's in Sussex all this week,' James replied, just
as a small dressing-gowned figure appeared at the head
of the stairs.

'Mrs Shinway. . . Maud, you're not to come down!'
James went up to intercept her.

'I'm feeling better, Doctor, not dizzy at all. I heard
the phone go and I wondered. . .'

'No.' James shook his head. 'It was nothing about
Lou.'

Mrs Shinway saw me, 'Oh, Dr Kate. . .oh, what a
good thing you're here! I'll come down and make you
both some tea. I'm well enough to do that.' She didn't
exactly push James aside, but sidled past him, and was
in the hall before he was. She looked flushed and had a
cough. As she turned towards the kitchen, Clare

Archibald came through from the surgery quarters, stripping off her white coat.

'Any news?' She looked straight at James, then at me, as he shook his head. 'Hello, Kate.'

'Hello, Clare.' There was someone behind her—a little dark man in an overcoat that was much too big for him. I remembered Mr Shinway from Eloise's party, even before James introduced us. He had heard about Eloise at the hospital where he worked as a porter. He was clearly upset, but trying not to show it, and after a few words with James he went off to the kitchen to help his wife, and no doubt comfort *her*.

Clare Archibald went home, for there was nothing she could do, and she had her father to look after. The Shinways came back with the tea—Bob Shinway carrying the tray, and keeping an eye on his wife who was none too steady on her feet. He was setting it down on a low table when we heard two short, sharp barks.

'That's Rollo!' Once more James was tearing out of the room. The Shinways were staring at one another.

'Perhaps. . .' Mrs Shinway croaked then the dog bounded in, confident of a welcome, which he got in full measure from Mrs Shinway, while her husband and I went through to the back when James didn't reappear. He was out in the garden, and I guessed why: he was looking for Eloise, in the hope that she'd been not so far behind Rollo, but I knew from his face and the shake of his head that she was nowhere to be seen.

'I'm going to ring the police.' He strode past us, back into the house. 'See if there's any news, and tell them that the dog's come back. They asked me to report any development.' As he went to the phone, Rollo came out into the hall and nuzzled against his hand. James stroked him, fondling his ears. 'If only you could talk,'

I heard him say, then he got the police number, and I went into the sitting-room.

'I don't think Eloise went off of her own free will, Dr Kate,' Mrs Shinway said in a half-whisper, before James came back. 'I don't think she would have gone more than a few yards down the road, not on her own, that is. If only I hadn't. . .if only I hadn't left her, but I just sat down and sort of collapsed, and I don't know how long it was before I could get on my feet and look outside again. She could have been gone for perhaps half an hour—anything could have happened! I shall never forgive myself, never, Doctor. I feel it's all my fault.'

She didn't cry, I had an idea that Maud wasn't the crying sort, but I knew how fond she was of Eloise, and I understood how it was she was blaming herself, although she shouldn't be, because no one can help being ill.

When James came back from the telephone to report 'no news' the Shinways went up to their flat. The clock struck the hour—that *nauseating* clock—eight p.m. The lights were going up in the street, but when I got up to draw the curtains across the bay window James stopped me. 'Leave them. I don't like the feeling that I'm shutting her outside.'

'No, of course not—sorry.' My hand dropped from the cord, and when I turned round James was there beside me. Once more we stood and looked out. Dusk was falling—had it ever, I wondered, fallen more quickly? We could just make out the short driveway where Eloise had been left playing when Maud Shinway had turned dizzy and hurried inside.

'I'm going out again,' James's voice came thickly. 'I can't stop here doing nothing. I'm going to have

another look round. . .on foot—I shan't take the car.
Can you possibly stay for a couple of hours, in case the
phone rings again?'

'Of course, James. . .anything,' I assured him. What
I wanted most of all was to go with him, but it made
sense for one of us to stay in. I doubted, however, if
James would succeed where the police had so far failed,
but one look at his face told me it was pointless to try
to stop him. I knew, too, that if I'd had a child, and
she'd been out there lost, I would have had the same
reaction, the same blind compulsion to do something,
anything, other than sit and wait.

I followed him into the hall, feeling helpless and
afraid—afraid for him. I shivered. 'At least wrap up,' I
said. 'It's not all that warm.' He was shrugging on a
jacket, when the phone rang not two feet away. He
reached for it, snatched at it, nearly dropped it. I heard
my own stifled gasp. There was a chair; I sat—I couldn't
have stood—I sat, and watched, and listened. I sat, and
prayed all over again—*Please let it be good news*.

James's words came in jerks, impatiently at first.
'Yes, of course I remember you. . .yes, and your husband.' He sighed and I thought, Oh, dear, another
enquirer. Then suddenly he jarred against the hall
table, nearly capsizing it. '*You've got her there*! Oh,
thank God. . .thank God! And she's all right, you say?
But how. . .how on earth. . .did you say *Chesterfield*?'
Then, as the caller went on, he drew me up beside him
to listen, not that I could make out any words, only
that a woman was speaking. All that mattered, though,
was that Eloise was safe. . .she was safe. . .*she was safe*
. . .and being looked after by someone in Chesterfield.

She came on the phone to her father, and he was
gentle with her, sweet. 'Lou, it's all right, don't cry, it's

all right, it wasn't your fault. No one is cross with you, poppet, we're just glad you're safe. Now, I've got some news for you—Rollo is back. . .yes, he came in a few minutes ago. So be a good girl, do what Mrs Clements tells you, and I'll be with you in three or four hours. I'm coming to fetch you. . .yes, in the car, and no, I'm *not* bringing Rollo. He's caused enough trouble one way and another, you can see him when you get home. Let me speak to Mrs Clements again, she'll tell me how to get to her house. All right then, darling. . .yes, all right. . .bye-bye now, see you soon.'

Minutes later, he was telling us all—for the Shinways were back downstairs—exactly what had happened—he couldn't talk quickly enough. 'Lou thought she saw Rollo in the back of a removal van, four doors down from here. Evidently the Clementses, who moved two days ago, had a second load of stuff to be taken to their new home. The tailboard of the van was down, and Lou climbed up inside, only to find that the dog wasn't Rollo, and it jumped out past her. She was just about to follow when she heard the men coming back. She knew she shouldn't be in the van and hid in panic. The next thing she knew she was in darkness, the doors had been slammed to, and the van was moving; she fell over, and shouted and banged, to no avail. There was furniture all round her, she said, and she could hear a radio playing. I expect the men were in a cabin, up front, where most sounds would be muted. In the end the poor kid stopped shouting, and my guess is she fell asleep. Anyway, she ended up in Chesterfield at the Clementses' new house. When the removal men opened the van doors and let the tailboard down, a sleepy little girl was found, curled up on a couch!

'Heavens!' I said. The Shinways were dumb. Not so

James. Freed of anxiety, high on relief, he was on the phone to the police, telling them what had happened, thanking them for their efforts, telling them he was off to Chesterfield.

'It's a very long journey there and back,' I said, when he came off the phone, and I knew I was fearful for him again—all those miles. He wouldn't be back until the small hours, and underneath all that relief, that freedom from unbearable strain, was a very exhausted man.

'I'll come with you, sir, take a turn with the driving,' Bob Shinway put in, and this wasn't so much an offer of assistance as a statement of intent. 'You go back to bed, dear, and stay there.' He looked sternly at his wife, who agreed to do so. Mr Shinway, I realised, was a force to be reckoned with.

'And I'll ring Clare Archibald and feed Rollo,' I suggested, for I had to do something to help, even though I couldn't drive to Chesterfield with James, which I would have given my eye-teeth to do.

I went out with him to the car, while Mr Shinway took his wife upstairs, but before we reached it he turned and swept me into his arms. I felt my feet leave the ground, felt the wedge of his cheek slammed up against mine. I felt the jubilation in him, which conveyed itself to me, and we laughed for the joy of it, and kissed because of it, and it was then that I knew I loved him. . .loved him deeply. . .and I nearly told him so. Yet somehow, even then, I managed to hold the words back, although they still might have come tumbling out—recklessly, foolishly out—if Mr Shinway hadn't appeared, pulling on his driving gloves.

I stayed in the garden for a few minutes after they had driven off. I knew that I was going to have to break my engagement to Nick. My feelings for James were real and abiding, they had taken deep root. The fact that he didn't return them—simply fancied me, on and off—didn't mean that I could say, 'Blow him,' and marry a man whom I cared about, minded about, but didn't love with desperateness. And there *is* a desperation about loving, it involves so much. It *has* to be right if it's to last a lifetime—for better or worse. I didn't love Nick like that. . . I never, ever had. . . I knew that now, and was aghast at myself for making such a terrible, painful mistake.

The enormity of it, the thought of telling him, filled me with dread. What would he say. . .would he mind very much. . .was it too soon to tell him after his accident, and after his mother's death?

My common sense, or sense of fairness, told me the sooner the better, for he mustn't continue to plan a future with me at its centre. He would be back home on Sunday. It would have to be then. On Sunday afternoon I would drive over to Park Road and tell him. I felt sick at the thought of it, but knew it would have to be done.

I didn't realise I'd been walking up and down the lawn till I saw my sodden shoes, till Rollo joined me there, thrusting his nose in my hand. I hurried in then; I had things to do. I rang Clare Archibald first, then Aunt Laura to tell her about Lou, and to say I wouldn't be long. After that I fed Rollo with a tin of his food which I found in the fridge. Then I took Mrs Shinway a cup of Complan, took her temperature as well, dosed her with aspirin, and finally left the house.

CHAPTER ELEVEN

NATURALLY enough my aunt and uncle were all agog to hear an unabridged version of Eloise's escapade. Aunt Laura declared that I looked worn out and plied me with food, which just at that moment I had no real appetite for. There was no doubt about it—the strain of the last two hours was taking its toll, but as well as that—even more than that—the thought of Nick and the coming break-up filled me with nervous dread.

'If you don't eat, you can't work,' Aunt Laura said sensibly. She and Uncle had had their meal over an hour ago. 'You know that the child is safe now, and that James is on his way to her. You'll be seeing Nick on Sunday, remember; fix your thoughts on that.'

She could hardly have made me feel worse if she'd tried. I put down my knife and fork. Catching Uncle John looking at me—and, believe me, he was no fool—I was tempted to confide in him, to confide in them both—tell them I'd discovered I didn't love Nick enough to go through with our marriage, and would have to tell him so. But as I chewed hard on food I didn't want, I managed to keep my own counsel, to keep my lips sealed in other words, for it was hardly fair to Nick to tell anyone else before him. At least I owed him that.

In bed that night I rehearsed what I'd say to him. I did so hope it could be done without unpleasantness; I hoped we could part as friends. That particular phrase had always sounded corny to me, pathetic, even impossible, but now I knew how important it was, for I didn't want to hurt Nick.

I was still awake at three o'clock, when my thoughts turned to James. He would be back home now with Eloise, and the little ménage at Theodore Road would be complete once more. I thought of James twirling me round in the garden, I thought of the rough pressure of his cheek against mine, and the soft-hard sweetness of his kiss. I loved him so. . . I loved him. . .but much good would it do me! Oh, why did I have to fall in love with a man who couldn't be mine? I remembered him saying that Helen was in Sussex, so when would she be back? Doubtless if she had been at home yesterday she would have been at James's side, and I would have come away, I expect, feeling superfluous.

He rang me next morning, soon after breakfast, and somehow or other I knew it was him the moment I took the phone off the hook. 'Just to let you know we got back safely.' Even the sound of his voice was enough to put my pulse into overdrive.

'I thought of you.' I could admit that, surely. 'Did you have a terrible journey?'

'With Lou at the end of the first lap, and bed at the end of the second, I had a two-way incentive, so no, it wasn't too bad.'

'And Lou is all right?'

'As ninepence—she was up before me this morning.' There was a breathing pause, then he added, his voice sounding very close, 'Kate, thank you for what you did—for standing by, I mean. I was at my wits' end. I needed. . .someone.'

But Helen for preference, I thought. I hadn't missed that slight hesitation when he'd spoken the last few words. I was jealous, and I knew I was, yet some of this took itself off when he went on to ask me if I could come to tea tomorrow. 'Lou and I would be delighted if you could, if you've got nothing else on. I may even be able to persuade Mrs Shinway—who's feeling very much better—to make you a green jelly rabbit, all to yourself!'

I laughed somehow. . .managed to laugh. . .but knew I couldn't accept, for tomorrow was the afternoon when I was motoring over to Nick. I was geared for it, poised for it—I couldn't put it off. Nick would be back at the Park Road house at two o'clock tomorrow, Sunday, having had his lunch en route. He had told me all this yesterday morning, when he'd rung from his office in town. And apart from that, it just wouldn't do to keep letting things happen with James. I wanted them to happen. . .all of them. . .the ultimate, in fact. But there was Helen, wasn't there? And in no way, *none*, did I mean to become some kind of locum girlfriend while she was away, or busy in her surgery, filling cavities.

'You're not exactly jumping at it, are you?' It wasn't until James spoke that I realised I hadn't answered him. 'You don't *have* to come, you know.'

'Oh, James, sorry, I'm half asleep, not concentrating well.' I kept my voice light and airy, even laughed again. 'But tomorrow, I'm afraid, is difficult. Nick's coming home——'

'Say no more,' he interrupted, 'of course, I remember now. Sunday is the big day, isn't it? How could I have forgotten?' He didn't sound as though he minded being turned down. In fact, to my over-sensitised ear he sounded a trifle relieved. He had probably, I realised, only asked me to thank me for yesterday, and to be polite, for that is the way nice men operate.

It appeared, however, that he hadn't quite finished, for he went on to tell me that a case of wine—champagne, no less—had been sent to him by our one-time casualty patient, Mr Alex Raunds. 'It came here to me, but was addressed to both of us. There was a note attached—with grateful thanks and all the rest of it. He's keeping well, he says.'

'How good of him to send it!' My mind flicked back to my very first meeting with James—when I'd raised my head to gulp in air, and had seen him kneeling down, facing me across Mr Raunds' unbreathing, whale-like front.

'We saved his life. No doubt it was worth a case of champagne.' James sounded brisk and miles away again. 'When I'm in the River Road area, I'll drop your share in.'

'Thank you,' I said, then someone called him, and this effectively brought an end to our conversation, which was rapidly tailing off.

The champagne would please Uncle John, I knew, but it was a little ironic for me to have it now, with nothing to celebrate. You're feeling sorry for yourself, Kate Chalmers, snap out of it, I thought as I went through into the surgery and buttoned on my coat. I ought to count my blessings, good health being one of them. I glanced down the appointments list and saw that my first patient was a multiple sclerosis sufferer. She was only twenty-four, and walked with two sticks with the utmost difficulty; next year she'd be in a wheelchair. Being a GP was a great leveller, or did I mean 'balancer'? There was always someone whose absolute courage in the face of terrible odds made you see life in proper perspective, and once again I was oh, so thankful I had chosen medicine as a career.

Morning surgery took me up to eleven o'clock, then came more house-calls than usual, for the flu epidemic was taking a vicious hold.

Saturday was just as hectic, ending with a phone call from the receptionist of one of the small hotels in Lower Bridge Street. 'It's one of our weekend guests, Doctor. He's just arrived and is having a terrible nose-bleed. I've done all the right things, but I can't stop it, and there's blood all over the place!'

'Sit him down, lean him forward, put a cold pad on the bridge of his nose. I'll be with you in ten minutes,' I said, going out to the car.

One never knew with epistaxis. In the usual way it isn't serious, or not very often, and stops spontaneously. It could be very frightening, though, and fright raised blood-pressure, which has the effect of increasing the flow. I wondered if the patient was hypertensive, or had struck his nose somehow, or was another influenza victim, when nose-bleeding often occurs.

His name turned out to be Angus Brodie, and he'd been taken into a little room behind the office; he still had his overcoat on. His weekend case was down on the floor, and, contrary to what I'd said, the receptionist was holding his head *back*, making him swallow the blood, which he coughed up, making even more mess, and him more terrified. 'It looks worse than it is, Mr Brodie.' I shooed the receptionist off, not very politely, I'm afraid, especially when I found that she'd slipped one of the room keys, with the label still attached, down his back; what on earth was she thinking of?

With the help of the manager, who came fussing in, I got Mr Brodie down on the floor, propping his head and shoulders up with a chair. Then I nipped his nostrils, telling him to breathe through his mouth. 'And don't worry if, after five minutes, the bleeding hasn't stopped. I can pack your nose with ribbon gauze impregnated with a substance that will help the blood to clot. Either way we're going to win!' I tried the effect of a smile, which seemed to work, for during the five minutes' nose-nipping time he told me, in nasal tones, that he'd had a bad drive down. . . 'On the motorway, you know, Doctor. I godda bid worked up.'

'Which almost certainly caused this bleeding.' I was looking at my watch; there were two more minutes to go. 'Did your head feel tight?' I asked.

'Very budge so, but nod now.'

'Well, that's something,' I smiled. We were on our own, the manager having gone off on ploys of his own. Through the half-open doorway I could see the receptionist answering her phone. She was even fussing about that—flapping around for a pencil, picking up papers and dropping them. Perhaps she was new to the job.

The nostril-pinching hadn't been enough to arrest Mr Brodie's bleeding, so I packed his nose with ribbon gauze soaked with adrenaline. I was gentle about it, for noses are tender. 'That will do the trick,' I said. I took a blood-pressure reading, checked his pulse, and went with him up to his room. 'Rest on your bed for an hour,' I suggested, 'then you'll be able to go down to dinner. Don't attempt to remove the gauze yourself. Either I or Dr John Chalmers will be along tomorrow morning, to ease it out for you. Until then you'll have to breathe through your mouth, as you're doing now.'

'I'm going to have a job to eat and breathe at the same time,' he laughed.

'You'll manage it, I'm sure.' I warmed to him; he

was a very pleasant man—thin on top, bespectacled,
studious-looking and bloody-faced. He said he'd have a
wash.

Saying goodbye, and leaving him to it, I made my
way downstairs, missing a step and nearly falling when
I saw who was in reception—James with his medical
case at his feet, hands on hips, while in front of him the
receptionist and the manager appeared to be having a
row.

James looked up and saw me, the girl and the
manager turned round, and then I learned that we had
both—James and I—been called out for the same
patient, the luckless Mr Brodie. 'I rang Dr Masefield,'
the manager said, turning directly to me. 'That was why
I was rather surprised when a lady—when *you* arrived.
I assumed you were Dr Masefield's new partner, so
raised no query. Now I learn that Mrs Barr here——'
he looked daggers at the receptionist '—telephoned for
a doctor herself, and called you out. I can't tell you
how sorry I am, Dr Masefield——' he turned back to
James '—that you were called out for nothing, busy as
you are. I suppose——' he swivelled a little more and
addressed poor Mrs Barr '—that you haven't dialled
999 and called an ambulance as well!'

She declined to answer, and I didn't blame her; I
even felt sorry for her, or at least I did until she spoke
to James, and asked him, as he was here, if he would
like to go upstairs and check Mr Brodie over. James's
answer was swift, even more swift than my outraged
catch of breath.

'No, I would not,' he said pleasantly, 'for two simple
reasons. In the first place it would be unethical, and in
the second there's no need. Dr Chalmers here has

treated the patient, which means he's had first-rate care.'

He didn't look at me as he said this, but I felt a positive glow. I stood there, fairly basking in it, and when I left the hotel a few minutes later, with him at my side, I still had the feeling that I was floating two inches from the ground.

Our cars stood side by side on the forecourt—his long and black, mine small and bright blue, each a little hazy in the dusk. 'I've brought your wine,' James told me. 'When I was called out, I realised I'd be passing the Larches, so I loaded it into the boot. You may as well take it now, I'll put it in your car.'

'Thank you, I'll unlock it.' I did so, and waited for him to make the transfer. 'It can go in the back,' I said, opening the nearside rear door to its fullest extent. The bottles were safely stowed inside. I watched James's long back straighten as he drew his head and shoulders out of the tiny car. I knew I should move round to the driving seat, but somehow I just stood there, eyes looking straight ahead, fixed on his collar and tie.

'You look like a fairy princess from Grimm's,' he said softly out of the dusk.

It was my hair that prompted him to say this, I knew, for I had washed it earlier on, and, not expecting to be called out again, I had plaited it into a single rope, pulling it forward over my left shoulder. It hung to my waist; I felt him lift it, then lay it back again. As he did so his fingers brushed my breast, and a tremor shot through me, shocking in its intensity. I heard him say my name, quickly and with a catch in his voice, and then I was willing myself to step back from him.

'It was good of Mr Raunds to send us the wine.' My words came out stiltedly.

'You said that before.' He reached for my hand, his thumb caressing my palm. 'It's a shame we can't share it properly—drink it together, I mean. We could perhaps get a little tipsy in the process and forget everyone else but ourselves.'

'I think not,' I said, and he burst out laughing. Well, I *had* sounded rather prim. I laughed too, I couldn't help it, and once more we were back on common ground. . .on dangerous ground. . .magic carpet ground, that could whisk us away with no thought for the morrow, if we dared to give it a chance. 'I have to get back.' I looked full at him then, and I fancied that his eyes held love for me, but I couldn't be sure. It was probably all in my mind.

'I too.' He raised my hand and kissed my fingertips. I drew in my breath and jerked away. What was he trying to do—make me die of loving him, of wanting him? It was all I could do to stumble round the car and squeeze myself behind the steering-wheel.

Once there, it was fairly easy to say goodnight and move off, for another car was turning on to the forecourt and wanted my space. The wash of its lights picked out James standing there straight and tall, beside the Volvo, lifting his hand in farewell.

As I drove home I couldn't help wondering if the relationship between him and Helen might not be all that it seemed. He had flirted with me, and he wasn't the type of man to behave like that if he was in love with someone else, not at all.

I knew I hadn't discouraged him—well, not as much as I should—so he might have thought things weren't going well between Nick and me.

James was honourable, a decent man—I felt that as strongly as the pull of his maleness. I shivered a little and tried to control my thoughts, which were running amok, running wild, skidding up and down the slippery slopes of 'perhaps' and 'maybe', but by the time I reached the Larches all I could think of, once again, was my coming meeting with Nick.

Sunday dawned, a bright, clear day without a cloud to blemish the sky. All the clouds were in me, and to try to dispel them I spent the morning hoeing in the garden, while Aunt Laura cooked the lunch, and Uncle John went out to Bridge Street to unpack Mr Brodie's nose. He returned just after midday to say that all was well. 'He was full of praise for you, Katie, wanted to know if you were my daughter, said you had gentle hands.'

'That was nice of him.'

'I said you were my *right* hand.' Uncle seemed intent on boosting my ego. Perhaps he could see I had got a worry on.

'I can't think why Nick couldn't have left Hatfield earlier, and had his lunch here with us,' Aunt Laura said when she was dishing up. 'I suppose you *did* ask him, Kate?'

'Well, no,' I said carefully, 'he said he'd be stopping on the way somewhere, and I left it at that.'

'You're a funny girl, you really are! You know he's welcome here.'

'Yes, Aunt, thanks, I do know.' She was right on the point, I knew, of saying that I must bring Nick back to supper, then Uncle John intervened and scotched anything along those lines by telling her that the young don't want middle-aged fogies round their necks all the time.

I set off at two-thirty, driving easily and swiftly through the nearly deserted Sunday streets. I felt calmer than I thought I would be, just a little dry in the mouth. I seemed extra aware of the landmarks I passed—the hospital on my right, St Saviour's college, the University Library, the fountain on Market Hill, and the Catholic church chiming a quarter to three. Another half-mile would bring me to Park Road, and now I had to admit to an onset of nerves: my hands were clammy and left little marks on the wheel. By the time I drew up at Nick's gate, however, I had everything under control—on the surface, that was—I just wished it were over, and I were on the way home.

I walked up the path, which was stone-flagged, my heels making clacking sounds, and perhaps Nick heard them, or saw me coming, for before I reached the front door he had it open, and stood there holding it wide, standing back for me to step inside.

'Hello, Kate.' If anything, he sounded even more nervous than I felt.

'Hello, Nick. How are you?' We leaned forward and kissed, stretching out our necks self-consciously, feeling awkward and stiff. It was then that I saw, over Nick's shoulder, that we weren't alone, that there was someone there, through in the sitting-room—a girl with long, limp hair. It was Jane Aveling. . . *Jane Aveling*! I couldn't conceal my surprise.

'Good afternoon, Doctor.' She came towards me, tucking back her hair. There was no confusion about her today; she looked smiling, and happy, and pink. 'It's good to see Nick looking better, isn't it—looking so well, in fact?'

I agreed that it was, although I didn't really feel that he looked all that marvellous—at least he didn't, not at that moment; he was jittery and on edge. Jane said she must go, and he leapt to the door, swinging it wide once more. While they exchanged whispered words on the step, I went through to the sitting-room.

'Sorry about that.' Nick was back very quickly; he sat down facing me. He didn't, I noticed, attempt to embrace me, and he had the look of a man who had something to say, and I thought I knew what it was.

'Jane is a very nice girl.' My voice sounded loud in that quiet room.

'Yes, she is. She wrote to me when she read about Mother's death. The letter was forwarded on to me. I . . .wrote back, of course.'

'Naturally.' My mouth was dry.

'Yes, she was quite upset. She knew Mother, you see, from coming here to see me when I came out of hospital.'

'She would be upset.' I was taking all this in, very, very slowly.

'But I didn't know she was coming here today; she just turned up. She. . .is inclined to do that.' Nick was flushed and ill at ease, gripping the chair arms for dear life, sweat beading his upper lip. Looking at him sitting there, the epitome of embarrassment, I knew he was trying to tell me what I was trying to tell him. We both wanted out, we both wanted to end our engagement. So why on earth didn't he say so. . .or why didn't I? We could hardly sit here all the afternoon metaphorically wringing our hands, and avoiding one another's eyes. It was too ridiculous.

'Do you want to break our engagement, Nick?' I said over-loudly, putting the onus on him, which was very mean of me.

He jerked as though I had struck him, went white, then very red. 'It's not what you think,' he blustered, 'it's nothing to do with Jane!'

'Supposing we leave her out of it.' I met his eyes squarely. 'Do you want to break things off? That's all I want to know.'

'Well, yes, I'm afraid. . .'

'Don't be,' I said, 'because that's what I want too. I think we're unsuited. We're friends, I know, but we don't understand one another. We have difficulty, don't we, in seeing one another's point of view? That's no basis for marriage, Nick. We aren't in love, we just thought we were during those marvellous weeks in Gloucestershire.' My voice was shaking. I felt relieved, yet terribly upset. Ending things for ever is terrible, like bringing down an axe.

'I had *no idea* you were feeling all this!' The look of faint outrage on Nick's handsome face swung me from tears to hysterical laughter, which I managed to control by speaking again, very rapidly.

'If you need any help, Nick, I'm always around.' I was slipping off my ring. It practically fell off, because I'd removed the binding tape at lunchtime. I got up and put it into his palm as if handing him a coin.

'Kate, I'm sorry. We made a mistake——' his fingers closed over the ring '——but it's not easy breaking off.'

'No, it isn't, it's horrible.' I made my voice brisk. 'But let's be thankful that it's a mutual decision. At least neither of us is hurt.'

Yet each of us *was* hurt, just a little, and we both knew we were, which was probably why we both apologised when we said goodbye at the gate. It was probably why my throat ached, and why it felt as if it was housing a lump the size of a boulder, as I steered the car towards River Road.

CHAPTER TWELVE

IT SEEMED best to tell Uncle John and Aunt Laura as soon as I got in. They would want to know why I was home so soon, anyway, so I walked in on them at teatime and got it over with. Uncle John looked grave and said, 'Oh, dear!' Aunt Laura was upset. 'But Kate, I thought you were so well-suited!'

'So did we, at first, but we made a mistake.' I didn't give any details.

'I could see it coming,' Uncle said quietly, pursing his lips, and handing me a cup of tea the colour of bog oak.

'For heaven's sake, John, she can't drink that, it's been stewing for half an hour!' Aunt Laura took it and bustled out, leaving the door ajar.

'Are you very upset, Katie?' Uncle was wearing his doctor's face.

'More than I thought I would be,' I replied, 'but I know it's for the best.' I didn't trust myself to say any more. Uncle John was very kind. Even Aunt Laura soft-pedalled a bit when she came back with fresh tea and scones.

'I think it's a pity, but of course you know best,' was all she said. I managed to drink some tea and mumble my way through a scone, but as soon as I could I escaped to my room, where I shed a few silly tears, then recovered enough to ring Mother and Father at Berwick-on-Tweed.

Mother answered the phone; there was a background

din of music and yapping dogs. She listened to what I
had to say, then came in quickly with, 'Thank goodness
for that, Kate. Nick's not the right one for you. I know
you feel upset now, but I'm glad you had the sense,
both of you, to see the light before it was too late.
There's plenty of time for you to marry, if you want to,
of course, and meet the right man, but for pity's sake
don't try to compromise. *I'll* tell your father, you leave
him to me. Now, don't mope around. Set about getting
yourself a partnership in a decent group practice. You
can do exactly as you like now, remember; there's no
one to clip your wings. There's a lot to be said for being
in control of your own life, Kate. So go for it, darling;
you and I are fighters, we come from Border stock.'

Mother has astringent qualities that never fail to
work. They worked for me like a poke in the ribs, and
after she had rung off I felt very nearly happy. She had
done me a power of good.

On the following Tuesday, during the afternoon,
Uncle John had a visitor. I knew nothing about it until
after supper, for I'd been out on calls all the afternoon,
followed by evening surgery. I thought he seemed
rather *distrait* after supper, while Aunt Laura had the
look of a woman bursting with news she'd been warned
not to tell. There was an air of conspiracy about them.
What on earth was going on?

I found out after supper when Aunt Laura—still
simmering—went off to her Tuesday game of chess
with a patient in Bloomfield Road. I was just about to
go up to my room, when Uncle asked me to spare him
a few minutes. 'I've something to put to you, Kate.'

'Sounds like a proposition,' I said briskly.

'That's exactly what it is.' He bent down to turn the
gas fire higher; we were having a chilly April. He sank

back in his chair with a little plop. 'Rose Spender came to see me today, brought the baby for her triple jabs . . .lovely little girl. Rose dotes on her—so much so, in fact, that she's not coming back here after all; she wants to be a full-time Mum.'

'Good heavens!' I stared at him.

'It happens,' Uncle puffed. 'A strong maternal feeling can override everything else. She wants to terminate—or rescind, I suppose—her partnership agreement.'

'But. . .can she do that?' I stammered.

'Yes, I've agreed to it.'

'But what will you do?'

'Advertise for another partner to take her place—a lady doctor, GP-trained—someone like yourself.' He looked at me across the expanse of rug and coffee-table. 'Would you like to stay in Seftonbridge, Kate, or do you want to get away?'

'Do you mean. . .?' I was gaping, I knew I was; I could feel my mouth dropping open.

'Yes, I do, that's exactly what I mean. Will you take Rose's place, be my permanent partner? We'd make a splendid team. I like your manner with the patients, I like the way you work. The fact that you're my niece has no bearing on anything; I'd want you here anyway.'

'Uncle, I don't know what to say!' And I didn't, and yet I was flattered to be asked, pleased to be wanted, and a steady warmth that had nothing to do with the turned-up gas fire invaded my very bones.

'I don't suppose you do, m'dear, not right off. What I'd like you to do is think about it over the next few days. If you decide to join me, you could keep living with us *en famille*, if you liked, or on the other hand we could make a small self-contained flat for you up on the second floor. We never use those rooms now. We could put in another bathroom, and a little kitchen; it could be your own domain.'

'Uncle John!' I was gasping again, I could hardly take it in—a partnership *and* a flat tossed in my lap like a coin.

'Your aunt's all for it, bursting with excitement—you know what she's like.' He smiled indulgently, then as quickly went solemn. 'But I mustn't be tempted to sway you, I know that,' he said. 'You may want to practise elsewhere, perhaps nearer your parents. I mustn't try to influence you, especially now you're free, but this isn't a bad practice, you know, and Seftonbridge is big enough to accommodate both you and Nick without you running into one another, when you might not want to. I'm putting this very clumsily, but you know what I mean.' He looked a little embarrassed, and rubbed one of his knees.

'I think it's a fantastic offer—a terrific chance,' I said, 'but yes, I would like to think it over, just for a day or two.'

'Of course, Katie. You do that, m'dear. We'll say no more for the present.' Uncle reached for the evening paper, and I went up to my room.

Sitting there in a chair by the window, I mulled it all over. It was a superb offer, but ought I to take it? Was it the right thing all round? It wasn't Nick I was chary of running into so much as James, of course—James and Helen as a couple; but perhaps they were no longer that. And if they weren't, and as I was free myself, perhaps one day. . . Then I caught myself up. For heaven's sake. . .it was folly to think like that. Yet he *did* like me, he *had* turned to me, there *was* something between us—something special, something terrific. Surely he felt it too.

I liked to think that I didn't allow dreams of this kind to sway me during the serious time of trying to decide whether or not to join Uncle's practice. I simply tried to see his offer as a chance to do what I wanted, to have what I wanted—a career in caring. I could be content with that. It was what I had always wanted, more than anything else. And I loved Seftonbridge with its dreaming spires, its watermeadows and lawns. I loved the river with its ancient bridges of cool grey stone, and the famous Backs, and the countryside stretching out into the Fens. So why not stay here, why not settle here, why not join Uncle John? Two days later I told him 'yes' and the die was truly cast. Aunt Laura was almost as pleased as he was, and she immediately set about making plans for the conversion of the four second-floor rooms. 'We'll get Doris's husband to do the work,' she said. 'His charges are reasonable. Oh, Kate, I can't tell you how glad I am that you won't be moving away.'

On the day the partnership agreement was signed, Uncle John insisted that he and I must go out for a celebratory meal. 'Dinner at The Blue Boar,' he decreed, and at seven-thirty that evening there we were in the grill room, Uncle's favourite eating place.

The grill room was on the ground floor, the main restaurant one floor up, and as we sat at our table working our way through plate-sized steaks we had a splendid view of the diners going up to the main restaurant—or coming down it—as the stairs were on our right.

We were eating cheese—a very ripe Brie—which practicallly dripped from the knife, when who should

come sailing down the stairs on the arm of her husband
but Doris Leigh? She spotted us at once. She came
over, dragging Ron with her, both looking very smart—
Ron in a well-cut lounge suit, Doris in yellow, big hoop
earrings swinging against her cheeks. She looked well
and happy. 'We've been celebrating my good health,'
she laughed. 'I think you should mark these things,
don't you, not just take them for granted?'

'I couldn't agree more, Doris.' Uncle raised his glass
to her, so did I. 'And we, also,' he told her, 'are
celebrating tonight. Kate is now a member of the group;
she's my permanent partner. Rose wanted to leave
because of the baby, so now everyone has got what
they want, me especially.' He beamed, and patted my
hand.

'I'm glad,' Doris said, 'really glad. Now I shall look
forward to coming back all the more.' I could tell she
was genuinely pleased, but I couldn't help being glad
that she didn't—not right at that moment—say anything about my break with Nick, for I'd hardly got used
to it yet. I realised that she knew about it, for Aunt
Laura had already been in touch with the Leighs about
the conversion of my flat. 'So there are *three* doctors
celebrating in here tonight,' was what she did say,
pointing upwards to the main restaurant. 'Dr Masefield
and Miss Clifford are up there, waiters flapping all
roound them, food being flambéd at their table, wine
in a cooler! Of course,' she tempered, catching her
husband's warning look, 'they don't have to be celebrating, but it looked that way to me.'

'The Blue Boar is suitable for most occasions,' Uncle
remarked, as Ron helped Doris on with her coat, soon
after which they left us, looking back to wave goodbye
from the doors.

'The Leighs are a nice couple,' I said, forcing myself to speak. I had been shaken to the core by the news that James was upstairs with Helen. Now all I wanted to do was get up and go. . .go before they did, before they came walking down those stairs.

Uncle snapped a piece of crispbread and buttered it, then said offhandedly, 'I've never really thought that James and the Clifford girl would marry. I still don't, and I'm usually right about these things. I knew James's wife—a lovely-looking, warm-hearted young woman. Miss Clifford couldn't be more different, and in my experience men usually fall for the same type—I've seen it time and again.'

'You're getting into deep water, Uncle!' I tried to be flip about it, for perhaps he suspected how I felt about James, and I had to nip that in the bud. 'In any case, it's none of our business, is it?' I managed to smile at him.

'As you say, my dear, none of our business,' he agreed, and ordered coffee. It was while we were drinking it, along with thimble-sized glasses of Cointreau, that I saw James and Helen coming down the stairs. They were laughing together, faces turned to one another—she blonde and petite in a strappy black dress that clung like skin, he lean and long in a dark suit, a rim of shirt cuff just visible as one of his hands trailed the banisters. She was carrying a fluffy white wrap, which he took from her arm and laid about her shoulders when they reach the foot of the stairs.

Uncle John had his back to them; I was facing their way. I willed them not to see us. . .please let them walk to the doors. I stared down at the tablecoth, wishing I could crawl beneath it, or dwindle in size, like Alice, and fall through the crack in the floor.

When no greetings rang over our heads, I risked looking again. They had moved; they weren't there, they were at the doors, pushing their way round them. I could see the paleness of Helen's wrap, the skimpy black of her dress, and James's hand in the small of her back, guiding her into the street.

They had gone; it was over, thank heaven for that! I swallowed some more coffee, and not a word did I say to Uncle John about having seen them. The thing was I couldn't trust myself not to show my feelings—not to show the jealousy that was like a pain inside me. I felt foolish too, and that was nearly as painful as the other. I felt a fool for having imagined, for one moment, that James and Helen Clifford were cooling off, and that he might care for me.

In bed that night I took myself to task, and faced up to the fact that now that I was a fully-fledged partner and would be in the district for years, I had to armour myself against James, just treat him as a colleague. I had to pull down the shutters on my feelings, and do so pretty damn quick.

Work helped, of course, work always does, and I had to admit that I felt happy and proud when my name appeared on the plate on Uncle's gate. There was such a difference between being a locum and being one of the firm. The patients really were *my* patients, not merely borrowed from Rose. They would come back to me, and back again; I would get to know them well. Several of the more chatty ones had comments to make—'I see you're a proper partner now'. . . 'Glad you're not leaving us' and. . .'I like Dr Spender, mind, but you understand my veins.'

Four days later I had a house-call to make, roughly a mile from the Larches. Mr Reenham, our patient, had moved house, but as he had no wish to change doctors we had kept him on our list. Strictly speaking he was within James's territory, so perhaps it wasn't surprising that, after I had made the call and was coming away from the house, I should see him some distance away, about to get into his car. He had plainly been visiting a patient too, for he was carrying his medical case. Once again I hoped he wouldn't see me, yet because he was alone I also found myself wishing that he might. My wish was granted with lightning speed. I saw him look up, hesitate for a second, then start to walk towards me. I stayed by the Renault, one hand on its roof, trying to look unconcerned, trying to remember my resolution to cut him out of my life.

He was wearing a light grey suit, its jacket undone, and I could see his shirt, see his blue tie blowing to the side. One arm was dragged down by his case, the other swung at his side. I saw all these things, and I filled up. I longed to run to him. But I had no right, he was Helen's, so I stood there glued to the spot, with my face stretched in what I hoped was a non-giveaway smile.

'Kate! Just the lady I wanted to see.' He grasped my hand and shook it. 'Congratulations on your partnership. I saw Dr John this morning, and he told me about it. I'm pleased for you. Very well done.'

His words, his touch, the way he looked at me, disarmed me all over again. I would never get over him, never, I would love him till I died. And this angered me. . .it made me angry with myself. How could I be so weak? 'I don't know that it's a case for congratulation,' I said. 'I didn't actually *do* anything, it just fell into my lap.'

'He also told me your engagement was off.' He was

looking at my left hand, which I quickly thrust into my jacket pocket, hiding its nakedness.

'He seems——' I laughed and tried to be airy '—to have kept you well-informed.'

A flicker of surprise, or bafflement, showed on his face for a second. I was overdoing the offhandedness, yet something egged me on—a kind of defence mechanism, perhaps, a last desperate bid to make him think I cared nothing for him, for how terrible it would be if he guessed the truth which I still felt must be written all over me. He'd be sorry for me, and so would Helen, and I couldn't bear that. I could only bear to face them, and meet them, if they had no inkling of what I was feeling. 'Marriage isn't for me, it doesn't appeal.' I looked him straight in the eye. 'I need to be free to control my own life; I don't want to be tied, I never did, and I'm not maternal, so there's no pull there.'

The silence that followed this spate of lies seemed to go on forever. We still held one another's gaze, but nothing was being conveyed. His eyes were as veiled as mine, then I saw his lips start to move. 'Feeling like that, I wonder you bothered to get engaged,' he said. 'It was hardly a fair thing to do when you never intended to see it through.'

The quiet censure in his voice flicked me on the raw. 'Oh, for goodness' sake don't preach,' I flared, 'and you *do* preach, James. I've noticed it before. . .it's boring!' I turned my back on him to hide my face and unlock the car, appalled at what I'd just said.

I felt his anger before he spoke; it seemed to clip my ears. 'I appear to have caught you at a bad moment,' he said. 'For that I apologise.'

It was for me to apologise. I'd been rude and offensive, and there'd been no need for that. But I didn't get a chance to say a word, for a woman with a baby hailed him from the other side of the road, and he went off to join her. He stood there with her, his back towards me—a grey broad-shouldered back, an eloquent back that spoke without words, that told me to get the hell out of it, to drive away and not bother him, which was exactly what I did.

I worried about this little episode for days afterwards. I thought of writing James a note to say how sorry I was, but in the end I did nothing, I decided to leave things as they were. I had accomplished what I had set out to do—driven a wedge between us, made it clear to him, by lying through my teeth, that I wanted nothing from him, that I didn't care a jot for him, or his opinions, nor did I hanker after him. By my very own hand, though, I felt I'd slaughtered something precious. Then I told myself this was all in my mind, and simply carried on. I was busy, which helped; I flung myself into my work.

What didn't help, however, was that during the following week I began to have toothache, a gentle nag in one of my upper molars, which wasn't unbearable, but it made me feel on edge, Uncle John was very concerned, and kept on and on about it. 'Make an appointment with Gregson's,' he said, 'or I'll do it for you. I know Jeremy Gregson; he may be able to fit you in very quickly. It's miserable trying to work like that, you musn't let it go on.'

'You will make sure it's with Mr Gregson,' I stipulated carefully. No way, no *way*, would I submit to Helen Clifford. In any case, my tooth wasn't all that painful; there were long periods when it was quiescent, so it might easily cure itself. But Uncle wouldn't be put off; he picked up the phone and got me an appointment with Mr Jeremy Gregson for Thursday afternoon.

So often, once the dread assignment with a dentist is made, the tooth stops aching, but with me the reverse was the case. It hardly ceased jabbing over the next two days. I was actually glad to walk through Gregson's front door on Thursday afternoon, and give my name at the desk. A Miss Leemur, who was one of Uncle's patients, was the secretary-cum-receptionist, and she had the worst kind of news for me—Jeremy Gregson was ill. 'He went down with this virus thing just before lunch. I've been cancelling all his appointments, but as you're in pain Miss Clifford will see you. She's got a patient with her now, but shouldn't be long, so take a seat.' She waved me to the chairs.

Swallowing my dismay, more than that, horror, I quickly shook my head. 'Oh, no, I don't think so,' I said. 'Oh, no, I couldn't do that. As my appointment was with Mr Gregson, I'll wait until he gets back.'

'But it could be a week, Dr Chalmers.' Miss Leemur looked surprised. 'Miss Clifford is an excellent dentist, she's very well-liked, *and* she has kept the next half-hour free for you.' Her voice held faint reproach.

Even so, I might have said no, might have walked back into the street, but my tooth chose that moment to give a violent leap. The truth hit me as hard as the pain; I couldn't do my job and feel like this for another week, so perhaps I really ought to swallow what I felt about her as a woman, and let her treat me. As if to reinforce this, she chose that moment to come out of her surgery with a patient in tow—a shock-headed man with a limp. 'Fit Mr Johnson in some time next week, a fifteen-minute appointment,' she said to Miss Leemur, then turned round and saw me there. 'Oh, good, you're right on time, Kate, come along in.' She smiled at me, and in I went, for what else could I do? If I refused treatment she would think I was scared, or doubted her competence. The first was true, and sprang from the fact that I knew she didn't like me, nor I her, so the basic trust one should have in one's dentist wasn't as strong as it should have been. I wasn't happy at all.

Yet people seem different in different settings, and here in her surgery, neatly gowned, professionally brisk, but sympathetic too, Helen Clifford could have been a stranger, another person altogether. 'Dental pain isn't funny,' she said, as she introduced me to her chairside nurse, then had a look at my tooth. 'It's a loose filling, a small one, but it's probably moved enough to expose the nerve. Your teeth, on the whole, are very good, you know. You've obviously taken care of them, I see you've only had two other fillings—not at all bad for your age. Now, what I'm going to do is give you an injection, get the old filling out and rebuild the tooth. Normally you wouldn't need an injection for a filling of this size, but as the tooth is painful. . .'

'You can say that again,' I managed to voice, just before she approached me with the syringe. Her hands came close; I remembered them, delicate little hands. I discovered they were skilful, gentle hands; I hardly felt the needle. After that it was plain sailing, although I have to admit that with the drill whistling inside my head I had one or two panicky moments. She wouldn't let it slip, would she? Well, no, of course she wouldn't. She was wearing her mask, her face was near mine, her eyes very intent, looking into my mouth, not at me, looking at my tooth. She was going to marry James, this wielder of the drill. . .or at any rate I assumed she was, and so did everyone else, apart from Uncle. I clung to that. Oh, if only the drill would stop. It did, at exactly that moment.

'I'm filling it now,' she said, taking little snippets of amalgam from a dish the nurse held out.

There was no noise in my mouth now, and no pain either. 'Bite gently together,' Helen said, then asked me how it felt.

'All right, I think.' I felt relieved and grateful. My face felt weird, of course—lopsided, heavy and useless, as though I'd had a stroke. The nurse placed a glass of mouthwash on the stand, and I rinsed out the bits. She removed my bib and left the room, and I sat up in the chair, while Helen wrote up my details at a small desk near by.

It was then that I saw the ring on the third finger of her left hand. It was gold and it gleamed, fashioned in the shape of two clasping hands. It was exactly the sort of ring I would imagine James would choose. So it was true, then, they *were* getting married, it wasn't just an affair. The sight of that ring pierced me; I couldn't stop looking at it. She finished writing, then turned to me, holding out my card. 'Give this to Miss Leemur on your way out, and don't chew on that filling for another two hours at least. It should be OK, but if you have any trouble, come back, of course.'

'Thanks, I will.' But all I wanted was to get out of the room. She seemed in no hurry to be rid of me, though, and mentioned my partnership.

'I heard about it from Jeremy Gregson—your uncle had told him. I expect you're pleased.' She stripped off her mask and flung it in the bin.

'Yes, I'm delighted, naturally. It's good to be settled, especially in Seftonbridge. I've always. . .liked it,' I was practically stuttering. We were both standing, and I felt huge beside her. I began to edge to the door.

'I think James told me you and your fiancé were going to live in his mother's house in Park Road. It's a very nice area.'

'We were, at one time, but Nick and I have split up,' I said. 'We decided we weren't right for one another. It was all very amicable.' I wondered that she hadn't known this, but then I supposed James and she had better things to talk about than me and my affairs. She looked surprised, even startled, her eyes becoming sharp with that hard blue flash I remembered from my very first meeting with her.

'I *see*,' was all she actually said, and I thought she would leave it at that. In fact I was practically to the door, when I heard her ask, 'What went wrong, Kate—did you fall for someone else?'

'I fell for my career,' I replied, smiling as well as I could with half my top lip drooping. I turned round to face her again. 'I found. . .find. . .that practising medicine is my first love, after all. I don't want all the trappings of marriage weighing me down.'

'I see,' she said again, still staring at me hard. The breeze from the window teased a tendril of hair from her bob. She smoothed it down and the gesture reminded me of Nick. 'Well, I hope you've done the right thing, that you won't live to regret it. I, now——' she fingered her ring '—I'm all for marriage myself. I'd hate to grow old without a man's protection and support. But I suppose I'm lucky, I mean, to be marrying into the medical profession, because I won't have to give up dentistry; I shall have the best of both worlds.'

'Oh, quite,' I said, and now I was well on top of the

situation, so much so that I actually asked when the wedding was to be.

'On the twenty-fourth of June, at twelve noon, here at St Peter's Church, so not long now, only seven weeks. Of course there's a lot to do, and arrange, and so forth.'

The nurse came back then, and I made my exit along the corridor to Miss Leemur's desk, to sign the forms and pay my bill. They were going to be married. . .they really were going to be married. Well, of course they were, that was why they'd been celebrating in the Blue Boar the other night.

'Injections make you feel a little dazed, don't they?' Miss Leemur said sympathetically, after she'd asked me—perhaps two or three times—if I had any smaller change.

But at last I was out of that building. I was out and walking home, and thank goodness I hadn't brought the car, for I doubt if I could have got it through the town centre, feeling as I did. Yet, why was it such a crushing blow. . .why was it such a surprise? Right from the start I had known that James and Helen were close. There had been plenty of indications that they might end up married. The child had mentioned it. . . 'When Daddy marries Helen I shall go to boarding school.' Aunt Laura had hinted at the same thing—'A doctor should be married.' Only Uncle John had thought that the liaison might break up. Well, he'd been wrong, hadn't he, very wrong? And now I realised just how very *desperately* I had hoped he might be right.

I would never get over James, never! There would never be anyone else. I went walking on, walking home, moving stiffly and mechanically like a clockwork toy that someone had wound up.

CHAPTER THIRTEEN

ON TUESDAY Uncle developed a cold, which alarmed Aunt Laura till I assured her that it wasn't the start of pneumonia, and wouldn't carry him off. It was a simple head cold, a coryza, but it made him feel less than his best. I took both morning and evening surgeries, and he went up to bed in the early evening, sniffing and blowing, filling the house with raucous explosions. It's a well-known fact that men never sneeze quietly.

'Remember, if there's a night call, you're not to turn out,' he instructed, as I took his temperature and found it to be only a shade above normal, which annoyed him just a bit.

'So, what do I do?' I shook down the mercury. 'Let the patient suffer?'

'*I* can go out, I'm not that ill—you've just told me so. Stick to the rule we made, and be sensible.' He lay back and closed his eyes.

I went out of the room, making way for Aunt Laura, who was bringing in hot lemon and honey, and oodles of sympathy. Our rule was that after midnight I didn't go out on house-calls. Uncle insisted that this was his job. 'We live in a strange world,' he'd said, 'women shouldn't be out on their own in the small hours, even women doctors; it's taking too much of a risk.' Personally I'd thought he was over-reacting, but of course I hadn't argued. As senior partner, Uncle John made the rules.

We seldom got a call after midnight, but that night

we did. The phone rang at twelve-twenty, right against my ear. I had taken the precaution of switching it through to my room when I came to bed, for, rule or no rule, if something came through, and it sounded urgent, *I* was the one who would turn out. A fine thing it would be if Uncle John infected a sick patient with his germs.

The caller was a Mrs Connerton; her husband was in great pain. 'Agony, Doctor, he's been sick and he's sweating, I think it's his stones again. I'm sorry to ring you at this time of night, but I can't stand seeing him suffer, and it's such a long time till morning, and. . .'

'Don't worry, I'll come——' I kept my voice low '—just give me the address.' I jotted it down—the Willows, Rushton Way—quite a long way out. To get to it I would have to drive past James's house, then on from there, over Leas Bridge to the part of the river where the rowing crews practised their strokes; I had never been there at night. Still, there was always a first time, wasn't there? I swallowed my dismay. 'I'll be with you. . .' I calculated swiftly '. . .in about fifteen or twenty minutes.'

Mrs Connerton's thanks were still ringing in my ears as I pulled on jeans and a sweater, and, carrying my trainers, made my way downstairs. I crept into the surgery to pick up my case and the patient's medical notes. A swift glance at the notes under the desk lamp told me that Ian Connerton was subject to renal colic, and most likely this was what he was suffering from now. I put the drugs I would need into my case, then let myself out of the house, praying that I hadn't awakened either my uncle or aunt. But no light flicked up at their window as I sped across the lawn, over to the garage, and lifted up the door.

A few minutes later I was off and away, driving in the direction of Theodore Road, which meant James to me, and I supposed it always would. It was a dark night with no moon and little traffic about. I couldn't resist a sideways glance at his house as I passed it. There was one lighted window—the living-room window; he was sitting up late, but then perhaps he always did. I didn't really know many of his habits, did I? He might be one of those men who could make do with very little sleep.

I put on speed, drove past, reached Leas Bridge, was over it and cruising down the other side in under fifteen minutes. I slowed when I reached Gorham Road, for Rushton Way was a turning off it roughly halfway down. I found it; it was poorly lit, and I couldn't drive to the end as the road surface wasn't made up, and I feared for the car. I got out and walked, lurching through the potholes, stumbling in my haste. A dark shape streaked in front of me, then another—two courting cats. I could hear them yowling in the bushes, see their crouching shapes. Then the house I was looking for came into view, and with eyes that by now were adjusted to the darkness I saw a woman at the gate. As I drew nearer I saw that the house was a bungalow, and the woman had a torch which she quickly flicked on. 'Are you the doctor?' she enquired anxiously. I told her I was, and she led the way, talking in low tones. 'I'm so glad you've come. . . I'm so worried about him!' She was a tall, angular woman in trousers and a checked shirt, her hair as long as mine.

The bedroom was to the right of the hall, she went straight in, leaving me to follow, I pushed the front door to. 'This is the doctor, Ian,' she said, as I went to the bed.

He was a big man, ashen-faced, his fair hair dark with sweat. 'You're new.' His voice came out in a gasp.

'Fairly new, yes.' I took his pulse, which was racing. 'How long have you been like this?'

'Since just after tea, round about seven,' his wife answered for him.

'Started suddenly, got a lot worse.' Mr Connerton's face contorted. I turned back the bedclothes and examined him briefly, disturbing him as little as possible.

'It's likely to be another calculus—another stone,' I explained. 'It's trying to get out of your body, giving you this pain in your loin. It's a nasty pain, I know that, one of the worst you can have, but I'll give you something to ease it and relax you generally.'

I injected pethidine into his arm, while Mrs Connerton filled a hot-water bottle, and placed it at his back. Next she laid a cool flannel on his forehead. She did both these things without any prompting, and when I left the bedroom some ten minutes later her husband was already falling into a doze. 'When he wakes,' I said, 'get him to drink as much as he possibly can. 'It'll all help, it's part of the treatment. I'll come and see him tomorrow morning before I start surgery. The injection will last until then and keep him comfortable.'

'It's good of you, doctor, coming out here like this. I thought it would be Dr John. I didn't realise, didn't expect a young lady; I thought. . .'

'I'm his partner—we take it in turns,' I said, not liking to tell her that Uncle John was indisposed. GPs aren't supposed to get ill, they're supposed to generate some magic potion into their bodies which keeps them in perfect health. No patient would ever forgive their doctor if he fell ill, for that was *their* prerogative. His job was to get them well.

I was anxious to get home, but it pleased me that I'd been able to help Mr Connerton. As I trudged back along the uneven road to my waiting car, I brought to mind the words of my senior partner at Cheltenham. 'A doctor can't work miracles,' he'd said, 'all he can aim to do can be summed up in three short lines,' and he'd quoted them to me. . .

> To cure sometimes
> To relieve often
> To comfort always.

I had never forgotten those words of his, and perhaps it was because I was thinking of them, and not of the dark, or the loneliness of the road, that I forgot my dislike of it, forgot my fears, and had no premonition of danger until I was getting into the car, when a group of youths leapt out of the trees and began to cat-call, 'Out late, aren't you, love. Looking for some fun?' One of them tried to grab me, but I got the door closed and locked in the nick of time, nearly leaving my leg outside. The grabber hammered on the window, the others did the same, then they jumped up and down, surrounding the car, shouting obscenities.

I knew I must start the engine, I knew I must drive off. . . I knew that. . . I knew that, but they gave me no chance. Before I could get the key into the ignition, they started to rock the car. They rocked it from one to the other of them, three of them on each side. . .rock-and-rock. . .rock-and-rock. . . I thought I was going to die. I tried to brace my feet under the pedals, I tried to hang on to the wheel, but I slipped and slithered, and could grasp nothing, I screamed, I could hear myself. Then by luck, sheer luck, the heel of my hand came down on the horn. The sound split the air, and the car stopped rocking, and I knew the boys had gone. I didn't see them go, but I knew they had gone. I couldn't see anything. I was dizzy and sick, I was terrified and bruised. I could do nothing at all but lie across the seats and wait for the queasiness to pass.

The sound of the horn had alerted no one, for there weren't any houses for another hundred yards or so. . . Supposing the boys came back. Supposing they were only just lying in wait. . .waiting to rock me again. I must start the car, *I had got to start it*, I must switch on and drive off. But I couldn't find the keys. I scraped over the floor and found them down by my feet. I still felt ill, my head still swam, I still had the sensation of seasickness, of swaying from side to side. I couldn't get the key in, couldn't switch on; the dashboard loomed like a screen, then dwindled into a narrow strip. . . I couldn't get the key in. But I had to keep trying, I had to do it, or the boys would come back, and the next time they might rock the doors open and drag me out on to the grass. The thought of that spurred me, cleared my head; fear guided my hand and the key went in, the engine springing into life.

I was steadier now, I could drive, I knew; I was going to be all right. I turned the car towards Gorham Road on the watch, all the time, for the boys. If I saw them I'd charge through them, blaring hard on my horn. Gorham Road was awash with lights, and the glow of the town lay ahead. I was safe. . . I was safe. . .and the thought of this kept me going for a time. I felt in control as I crossed Leas Bridge into Milands Lane, which led into Theodore Road with its gabled Victorian houses. James lived in Theordore Road—this thought entered my head as though it were new and something to be wondered at; perhaps I was going mad. My legs felt weak, my feet numb on the pedals; reaction was setting in, reducing me to a jelly again, all my fear came back. Even so, I don't think I would have braked and stopped outside James's gate if I hadn't seen that the light was still on down in the sitting-room. It was the light that drew me, the light that beckoned, for it meant that James was still up. He would help me, I knew he would, he would take me in, and shut the door, and I'd be all right. I had to go to him.

I got out of the car and up the path. I mustn't bang on the door, or I'd wake the whole house; I walked over the garden and tapped on the window—the lighted window—and heard Rollo bark inside. I'd forgotten Rollo, what a noise he made. Perhaps I shouldn't have come. Perhaps, even now, I ought to go, get back to the car. But my legs wouldn't carry me, my arms felt weighted, and I was still standing there with my feet in a flower-bed when the curtains parted, and I glimpsed James's startled face looking out. He dropped the curtain, was lost to view, then light spilled on to the steps, and he was with me, beside me, holding me up. 'Kate, whatever——! *Kate*. . .what's happened?' I heard the alarm in his voice.

'It's all right, I'm not hurt, there's not been an accident.' I strained to see his face, but kept slipping down the front of his sweater; he gripped me more tightly still.

'Put your arm round my waist, let me take your weight. . .into the house, keep going!' My legs were working, but I clung to him, I could hear myself explaining all that had happened as we went up the steps, as we entered the narrow hall, and so into the sitting-room, James uttering soothing words.

The light in the sitting-room was very bright; he sat

me on the settee. The cushions received me cloud-soft. I blinked up at him. 'My darling, are you hurt? I know you said not, but if you are you must tell me.' His voice was urgent, and he'd called me his darling. I smiled at him, thinking of that.

'I'm just bruised, that's all,' I assured him; he was smoothing the hair from my face. I was all hair, it was everywhere, having shaken free in the car. 'I was bounced about like a pea in a pod—a very loose pea!' I thought I could joke about it, but what a mistake that was, for I began to shiver and my teeth chattered, and the next moment James was folding my fingers round a glass and guiding it to my lips. 'It's brandy, it'll steady you—drink it down, every drop.'

There seemed to be a great many drops, but although I spluttered and choked I got it down. I had no option, for James's other arm was clamped about my shoulders. He meant to be obeyed. 'I shall be over the limit—to drive home,' I protested, but he shook his head, as though this was of no account or importance.

'What I can't understand,' he said, 'is how you came to be out on a call in the small hours of the morning. Rose Spender never went out after midnight; that was one of your uncle's rules.'

'It still is.' I giggled a little, for the brandy was getting to me. 'It still is, but he's got a cold, so I flouted orders and sneaked out like a thief in the night. It wasn't difficult.'

I expected James to laugh, but he didn't move a single laughter-muscle. He even frowned and looked quite fierce. 'You could have rung me,' he said, 'I'd have stood in for you, or rather for your uncle. We've always helped one another out.'

'I know, but I couldn't ask you.' I felt his arm leave my shoulders.

'I wonder why.' His voice had an edge, it was very nearly sharp. 'Why wouldn't you let me help you?' he asked, a little more gently.

I looked at him, and decided to tell him, for this was my chance to make amends, to put something right that had bothered me for days. 'Well, I'd been rude to you, hadn't I? Offensive and rude, saying that you preached and were boring, and of course you're not, and I knew it wasn't true. I wanted to apologise, but I never did, and that. . .stopped anything else.'

'Like asking a favour?'

'Yes, that's right, exactly like that.'

'Yet you're here now, you came to me.'

'Yes.'

'So, why was that?' He was giving me no quarter, and he seemed so remote. Oh, blow him. . .blow all men! What did he want from me, blood?

'Because I'd reached the end of my tether,' I gasped. 'I'm not brave like Helen. I can't shrug things off the way she does, so that's that, I'm afraid!' I was very nearly being rude again, then, meeting his eyes, looking straight into his *dear* face, I felt all my defences crumble, and I told him the truth, the simple truth. 'I just wanted to be with you,' I faltered. And then I was in his arms.

'Was that so difficult to say?' He kissed my open mouth, and my breath went, and I couldn't answer, except by kissing him back. And now a different kind of weakness was turning my bones to water, was drowning my resolve, my will-power, my sense, though perhaps some remained to taunt or haunt me, for I pushed hard against him and he let me go at once.

'I think you're. . .*we're* forgetting Helen!' I lurched to my feet and so did he, and even then I all but turned to him. 'It's my fault, James, I shouldn't have come, but I'm all right now. I can drive; I'll go, I shouldn't have come!' I began to move to the door with my eyes fixed on it, nearly tripping over Rollo, then I felt James's hand on my arm.

'I'll drive you home, Kate, whenever you want, there's no need to run from me—but first——' we were sitting down again '——first I want to know why we have to remember Helen. Where does she come in?'

As if he didn't know, I thought. Once again he was making me say everything, making me spell it out. Not that I cared now, for this was truth-time; the bit was between my teeth. 'It's about you being engaged to her. I don't make a habit of making love with other girls' men, not even when I've just downed a glassful of brandy!'

'I'm sure you don't.' He looked amused, and I felt like pushing him again, but what he said next was so unexpected that I nearly fell off the settee.

'Helen isn't engaged to me, Kate. She's engaged to a dentist in Sussex.' He was looking at me gravely now, his eyes moving over my face.

'To a dentist in Sussex. . .not to you?' Had I heard aright?

'No, not to me.'

'But I thought. . . I mean. . .everyone said. . .'

'People have that tendency,' James said a trifle cryptically, taking my hands in his, 'but so far as Helen and I were concerned, perhaps it was understandable that people paired us off. At one time we talked about marriage. I was vulnerable just then. I had lost Colette, missed married life; Helen was. . .sympathetic. Things didn't work out, though, in the long-term. There were issues we couldn't agree on, differences in outlook that would have made marriage a virtual battleground. At the time of the Roseveares' party we hadn't met for over three months, but I was pleased to see her, and she me. It was good to know there were no hard feelings, that we could meet and talk as friends. You probably know what I mean by that?'

I nodded, for I thought I did. I could look upon Nick as a friend now, and what a relief that was.

'When I mentioned that I was visiting my parents that weekend,' James continued, 'she asked if I could give her a lift to Brighton, where she was booked to attend a dental seminar. It was when she was down there that she met Stephen Bridewell, who has a practice in Hove. When she marries him she'll go into partnership with him. She's over the moon about it all.'

But it's you she'd rather have, I thought, bringing to mind our conversation in her surgery, the gist of the words she'd used. Now I might be doing her an injustice, and I might easily be wrong, but I was as sure as I could be that Helen had meant me to think it was James she was marrying. She had led me a few yards up the garden path, just for the hell of it. Basically she wasn't a kind person. James had had a lucky escape.

'Thank you for telling me,' I managed to say.

'It seemed to be necessary.' His eyes still looked amused, and I felt my face go red.

'She's a very good dentist; she filled my tooth. That's when I saw her ring, and she told me she was getting married soon.'

'She told me ten days ago, I took her out to celebrate.'

Yes, at the Blue Boar, I thought, but didn't say so

out loud. I began to feel happy, deliriously happy, but
as well as that a paralysing shyness had me in its grip. I
couldn't look at James. I looked at the clock, and said
I ought to go. Seeing some papers lying on a chair, I
even apologised for interrupting whatever he'd been
doing when I'd tapped on the window-pane.

'I was preparing a talk I'm giving to a group of
students at the weekend, but I'd nearly finished, so
don't worry about that.' Even he sounded stilted now.
He drew me to my feet, zipped up my anorak, arranged
its collar, and kissed me between the eyes, holding my
hair in a bunch at the back. 'Come on, I'll run you
home. We'll use your car, and I'll walk back afterwards;
it'll help me collect myself.'

I said nothing—I couldn't—and anyway he was
hurrying me from the room, shutting the door behind
us, shutting Rollo inside. My little blue Renault still sat
at the gate, just visible in the dark. I gave James the
keys, and he let me in first, then I fastened my belt,
watching him walk round the front of the car, feeling
the movement it gave as he got inside and slid behind
the wheel, 'It's a tight fit,' he joked, and I laughed, and
felt easier, and so, I was sure, did he.

On the way home he asked me about my break with
Nick. 'Did you decide not to marry him because you're
against marriage itself, or because you didn't want to
marry *him*?' The car purred gently on. I could hear my
own breathing, see James's hands resting on the wheel.

'That's a very direct question,' I parried. My heart
was beating faster. . .faster and faster. Why did he
want to know? 'I found,' I began, 'that I didn't, after
all, want to marry Nick, and it wasn't only that he
didn't want me to work, it was something far deeper
than that. I cared for him, but not enough, and as it

turned out he was having second thoughts too, so in the end it wasn't too difficult to part.'

'Thank you for telling me.'

'You asked.'

'I know.' He was stopping the car. We were on the home side of Garrod's Bridge, I could see the reflection of lights on the water flowing down to the weir. 'I had to ask, Kate.' He jerked on the handbrake, switched the engine off. 'I'm in love with you, I love you to distraction, and I have done for a long time, ever since I first clapped eyes on you in Rastners cocktail lounge.'

'*James*!' Our seatbelts held us apart, so we each snapped ourselves free, turned to one another, and I took his face in my hands. 'James, you must know that I love you too—to distraction as you said! I've loved you ever since that day I painted by Challoner's Bridge!'

'And left your ring in the back of my jersey. Oh, my dear, darling girl.' His kisses were soft on my eyelids and brow, on my cheeks, and nose, and chin, and when our mouths joined I soared again on that wing of delight, that singing joy which was part of my love for him.

'To be able to say, "I love you" is bliss,' I said when I could speak. 'I haven't known how to hide my feelings; I had to lie and be rude.'

'That's all in the past.' He caressed my cheek. 'Kate, will you marry me? I'm almost afraid to ask, for perhaps you still don't want to be tied, and there's Eloise—you may not like a ready-made family.' A little uncertainty slowed his voice.

But not mine. I was certain—sure and joyous. I folded my arms around his neck. 'I *shall* like it. . .all of it,' I said. 'I'm already fond of Eloise. In time I shall grow to love her, and of course I'll marry you. There's nothing in the world I want more than to spend the rest of my life at your side.'

'My dear love. . .my sweet Kate.' His voice throbbed close to my ear, making all the sounds I liked, whispering endearments. 'I know what you feel about your career, and I'll never restrict you, you know. You can practise medicine forever and a day, if that's what you want. It would be very strange if I didn't understand, being a doctor myself.'

We managed to get to the Larches, managed to part at the gate, but when I let myself into the house and crept upstairs to bed I reflected on how extraordinary it was that in a matter of less than three hours I'd been out on a call, been terrorised by boys, become engaged to James, while my aunt and uncle had slept on, completely unaware that I had taken one step outside my bedroom door. I thought only of James after that, and when at last I slept it was to dream of him proposing to me, all over again.

People's comments on our engagement were varied. Uncle John was pleased, Aunt Laura confused, Mother—over the phone—said, 'Thank goodness for that. . .he's a lovely, lovely man!' Father, thinking of Helen, had a job to take it in, but was glad he could still come south for my wedding, with all the family around.

We were married on Independence Day, Tuesday, the fourth of July. We had a brief honeymoon in Scotland, then came back to our work. I stayed on as Uncle John's partner, of course. It wasn't all that far to drive to the Larches, and the arrangement worked very well.

Mrs Shinway took charge of things at home, and little

Eloise continued as a day pupil at St Mary's School, Silver Street. 'I never really wanted to board there,' she confided to me one day. 'I just said I did, but it wasn't true, Katie.' I told her I understood.

I love Eloise and I know she loves me, but I want my own child one day—a boy, perhaps, who'll be just like James; twins would be ideal. Uncle John, who always looks ahead, and believes in facing facts, said that he was resigned to my wanting to work part-time one day. 'We'll co-operate, Kate, work in with one another. After all, I can't complain. Right from the very first I hoped that James and you would marry. I had my fingers tied in a knot from the night of the Roseveares' party.'

When I told James this, he fell about laughing, then was suddenly serious, as he looked into my eyes and said, 'He's the best GP I know.'

— MEDICAL ♥ ROMANCE —

The books for enjoyment this month are:

GYPSY SUMMER Laura MacDonald
THE BECKHILL TRADITION Lilian Darcy
THE DOCTORS AT SEFTONBRIDGE Janet Ferguson
A MIDWIFE'S CHOICE Margaret Holt

♥   ♥   ♥   ♥   ♥

Treats in store!

Watch next month for the following absorbing stories:

A PERFECT HERO Caroline Anderson
THE HEALING HEART Marion Lennox
DOCTOR'S TEMPTATION Sonia Deane
TOMORROW IS ANOTHER DAY Hazel Fisher

Available from Boots, Martins, John Menzies, W.H. Smith, most supermarkets and other paperback stockists.

Also available from Mills & Boon Reader Service, P.O. Box 236, Thornton Road, Croydon, Surrey CR9 3RU.

Readers in South Africa - write to:
Book Services International Ltd, P.O. Box 41654, Craighall, Transvaal 2024.

THE DOCTORS AT
SEFTONBRIDGE
by Janet Ferguson

We hope you have enjoyed reading this book. It is a new idea for the Mills & Boon Medical Romance series, a novel written in the first person seen directly from the point of view of the heroine, and we would like to know what you think about it.

Please spare a few minutes telling us your views and we will send you a FREE MEDICAL ROMANCE as our thank you.

Please tick the appropriate box for each question ✓

1. Did you enjoy reading THE DOCTORS AT SEFTONBRIDGE?

Very Much ☐   Quite a Lot ☐   Not Very Much ☐   Not at All ☐

2. **THE DOCTORS AT SEFTONBRIDGE** is written in the first person, which do you prefer, books written in the first person "I said" or books written in the third person "she said"?

I prefer books written in the first person ☐

I prefer books written in the third person ☐

I don't mind either ☐

3. Would you like to read more books written in the first person?

Often ☐   Occasionally ☐   Never ☐

4. Do you have any additional comments to make about **THE DOCTORS AT SEFTONBRIDGE?**

_____

_____

5. How often do you read Mills & Boon Medical Romances?

Every Month ☐   Every 2-3 Months ☐   Less Often ☐

6. Which of the following series do you read?

Mills & Boon:	Romance ☐	**Silhouette:** Sensation ☐
	Best Seller ☐	Special Edition ☐
	Temptation ☐	Desire ☐
	Duet ☐	**Loveswept** ☐
	Masquerade ☐	**Zebra** ☐

7. Where did you get **THE DOCTORS AT SEFTONBRIDGE** from?

Mills & Boon Reader Service ☐   New from the shops ☐

Other (please specify): _____

8. What age group are you?

16-24 ☐   25-34 ☐   35-44 ☐   45-54 ☐   55-64 ☐   65+ ☐

9. Are you a Reader Service subscriber?   Yes ☐   No ☐

If yes, your subscription No. is _____

THANK YOU FOR YOUR HELP
Please send your completed form to: Mills & Boon Reader Service,
FREEPOST, P.O. Box 236, Croydon, CR9 9EL

NO STAMP NEEDED

Please fill in your name and address to receive your FREE book:

Ms/Mrs/Miss/Mr _____ EDSB

Address _____

_____

_____ Post Code _____

You may be mailed with offers from other reputable
companies as a result of this application. If you would
prefer not to receive such offers, please tick box ☐